THE THOROUGHBRED

"Hello, Maura." Kevin's voice sounded softly in her ear. "We ride together at last."

What was it about Kevin that both attracted and infuriated Maura? True, he was strikingly good-looking, but she found his air of superiority irritating. The way he looked at her also upset her. It was as if he were trying to read her thoughts. His piercing eyes caused a stir in her that she had never experienced before.

"I imagine we'll be competing against each other," Kevin said. "And I intend to give you a run for your money."

The Thoroughbred

Joanna Campbell

BANTAM BOOKS
TORONTO · NEW YORK · LONDON · SYDNEY

RL 6, IL age 11 and up

THE THOROUGHBRED
A Bantam Book / November 1981

The Thoroughbred

Chapter 1

Maura Langdon had reason to be excited. As the low red sports car whizzed north into the rolling Connecticut hills, with her friend Jill Warren at the wheel, Maura thought of the two and a half months ahead. She was spending the summer on the sprawling horse farm owned by Jill's uncle. Instead of the few hours of riding lessons each week she was used to, she would be spending days in the saddle, jumping and hacking through the woods and across the fields.

The little car was held up momentarily in traffic, and Maura turned to Jill. "You're sure your father doesn't mind us taking the car for the summer?"

"It was Daddy's idea in the first place. He didn't want us to impose too much on Uncle Alex. Not that he or Aunt Lorna would consider anything I did an imposition. They spoil me like I was their child. I've been up here every summer I can remember."

Maura leaned her head back on the seat and smiled widely. "I can't wait to see the horses!

1

Just think. We'll be riding decent thorough-breds instead of stable hacks."

"Your father offered to get you your own horse," Jill reminded her.

"True," Maura mused, "but since dear old Maryvale has no stables, how often could I have ridden? Probably no more than I'm riding now, right? It wouldn't be fair to leave a prime hunter cooped up in a stall more time than he was out of it."

"That's my friend. Always thinking of the horses first," Jill said as she eased the little MG onto a narrow country road. "And once my uncle sees you ride, he'll put you on the best."

"You think so?"

"Come on, Maura, you're good. Compared to you, I look like a novice. No one would believe we'd taken lessons together for the last four years." Jill chuckled good-naturedly. "There'll be a lot of other things to do in Southbury too, besides riding—swimming, tennis, boys."

"Boys?" Maura repeated, wincing slightly.

Jill shook her head in mock disgust. "You know, Maura, just because Maryvale is a girls' school doesn't mean you have to live like a nun."

"I'd rather be riding."

"I know," Jill said. "But it's time you got to see that boys aren't the scary monsters you think they are. I'm gonna make sure that by the end of the summer, you're practically boy crazy."

"How're you going to do that?"

Jill winked mischievously. "You'll see."

2

Maura slumped back in her seat. For the next few minutes she gazed at the picture-postcard farms of central Connecticut and thought about her best friend.

Jill was petite, had short, curly reddish-blonde hair, and a dusting of freckles on her nose. She was talkative and friendly and could strike up a friendship standing in line at the movies.

How different I am from Jill, Maura thought. She was tall, with shoulder-length dark blonde hair. Unlike Jill, Maura knew she gave the appearance of being coolly sophisticated and, at times, snobbish. But she wasn't a snob, her reserve came from shyness. Also, she was a good student, while Jill got by on passing grades and took more of an interest in her wardrobe than her homework.

Although their looks and personalities were different, their backgrounds were similar. Their successful parents belonged to the same clubs, shared the same interests. As toddlers the girls had paddled in the same pool; later they had shared tennis, dance, and riding lessons.

Jill was a few months older than Maura, but they both had just finished their junior year at the Maryvale Young Women's Academy, where they were inseparable. Yet, despite their closeness, this was the first summer they were spending together.

Maura was an only child, and her parents had always kept her with them during the summer months, planning their vacations around her. And they had done a lot of things, Maura thought. One summer they had sailed along the New England coast; another they had visited Scotland, viewing the stark mountains, the old castles, and kilted bagpipers; and they had spent part of one summer in California, staying with friends in their Malibu beach house.

Yet Maura had missed having someone her age to share these vacations with. Now, for the first time, she was spending her summer with a friend, and she was going to be doing what she most wanted to do—ride.

Maura had loved horses since her first pony ride. She loved the challenge and the thrill of cantering across a field or toward a fence, gearing her mount's strides, feeling the muscle and power beneath her, then soaring upward like a bird, being one with the horse. She was proud she could clear a jump with inches to spare, land, and set out for the next, keeping the rhythm even. When on horseback, she had the unique ability of divorcing herself from the rest of the world. Only she, her mount, and nature's obstacles existed. She'd be in heaven this summer, and if she had her way, she'd spend all day on horseback. Despite what Jill had said, the last thing Maura needed was to get involved with boys.

Jill's voice pulled Maura from her contemplations. "For someone who's so excited, you're certainly off in a daze. We're almost there!"

"Are we?" Maura snapped back to the present and once again glanced out the car windows. There were huge old colonial houses on either side of the road, with acres of pasture land around them. They passed through the village center, with its grouping of stores, two restaurants, a bank, and more homes, set back from the sidewalk behind white picket fences.

A quarter of a mile beyond the village, Jill swung the car into a gravel drive. At its end Maura spied a stately white clapboard saltbox with green shutters accenting each of its many windows. Ancient, broad-limbed maple trees bordered the drive and stood as protective sentries on the green lawns. Behind the house were two rambling barns, riding rings, and in the distance, fenced pastureland as far as the eye could see.

Jill braked the car to a halt on the gravel. "What do you think?"

"It's fantastic! Why didn't you invite me before this?"

"Think your parents would have let you come?"

Maura laughed. "I had a hard enough time convincing them to let me come this year. They wanted me to go to Europe with them, but I really wanted a summer on my own—and the way this place looks, I think I made a good choice."

"So do I. When I was a kid, I really tried to con my parents into letting me live up here for a year—of course, I would have missed them and probably run back from homesickness—but it's great, isn't it?"

Before Maura could answer, the back door of the house flew open and a tall, middle-aged auburn-haired man strode out. He was dressed in riding chaps and boots. Walking to Jill's side of the car, he said, "Well, this is a surprise, you driving up in one of your dad's cars. You're growing up, my girl!"

"Uncle Alex!" Jill bounded out of the car and into her uncle's waiting arms. "It's good to see you. Where's Aunt Lorna?"

"If you turn around, you'll see her."

A slim, blonde woman was approaching the car. She, too, was dressing in riding chaps. A shining cap covered her short hair, "Ah, Jill." She planted a loving kiss on her niece's cheek. "We're so glad you're here!"

"Maura," Jill called. "Come and meet my aunt and uncle."

Maura quickly joined the threesome as Jill made introductions. "Aunt Lorna, Uncle Alex, this is Maura Langdon. Maura, my aunt and uncle, Mr. and Mrs. Warren."

Smiling, Maura extended her hand. "Mrs. Warren, Mr. Warren, thanks for having me here for the summer."

"It's our pleasure," Lorna Warren responded. "Jill's like our daughter. We're just delighted she's invited you. Come, I'm sure you're both ready for a snack. Alex, why don't you bring in their luggage while the girls and I chat."

The back door of the house led into a large kitchen, which, except for the modern stove, sinks, and refrigerator, was an accurate restoration of the low-ceilinged, huge-fireplaced room that had served the original owners in the 1800s. A long harvest table, surrounded by ladder-back chairs had been placed in front of the brick fireplace.

"Sit. Make yourselves comfortable," Lorna Warren said, indicating the table. "Cokes okay?"

"Sure," the girls replied.

Lorna went to the refrigerator and the cupboard and quickly returned to the table with the Cokes, a plate of cookies, and a cup of coffee for herself. "So, Jill, tell me all about your year. School go well?"

Jill shrugged. "I like it—just don't ask about the grades. I don't think Daddy was very happy."

Mrs. Warren grinned. "Well, you have other talents, though the schoolwork's important, too."

"Yeah, if I'm going to get into a good college without Daddy having to wedge open the door." Jill made an impish face. "But Aunt Lorna, I don't really know if I want to go to college. I don't know what I want to do."

"You will in time. Give it a year or two in liberal arts, then see if you don't find something. Your mother was a Smith girl."

"I think I'd rather go someplace else," she said. Turning to Maura, she added, "Some place with lots of boys."

"Nothing wrong with that." Lorna chuckled. "But it's getting an education that's really essential." She looked to Maura. "And have you any plans yet, Maura?"

"I haven't decided on a college, though I do plan to major in music."

"How interesting. Would you like to teach?"

7

"Probably."

"My sister was a musician—a pianist—though she does little with it now except to play for her own enjoyment."

"That's my instrument, too."

"It's too bad we don't have a piano here," Lorna said.

"It's okay, Jill told me," Maura said. "But you've got something I like even better—horses."

Alex Warren entered with the bags, the screen door banging shut behind him. "From the weight and amount of this luggage," he exclaimed, grinning, "I'm wondering if you plan on moving in permanently!"

"It *is* for the whole summer, Uncle Alex," Jill interposed. "And we'll help you." She rose quickly and grabbed a case. "Come on, Maura."

"Yes, go on up and see your room," Lorna Warren said. "We'll talk later after you girls have had a chance to unwind."

The old house had eight bedrooms in all, and the girls had been given a large back room overlooking the drive and stables. It had twin beds with ruffled white spreads, a large dresser, and an old-fashioned dressing table. A thick rose-patterned carpet covered the wide board floor. In one corner were a stereo and speakers, in another a comfortable wing-backed chair, and there was a fireplace along one wall.

"Oh, this is nice," Maura exclaimed.

"Homey, isn't it?" Jill said. "Thanks, Uncle Alex. We'll unpack fast. I know Maura wants to see the stables."

"A horsewoman, are you?" he said, turning his attention to Maura, who was lifting one case up onto the bed and releasing the catches.

"I love them, and I love to ride. I can't tell you how much I'm looking forward to being here."

"You've come to the right place. I can't promise any riding this afternoon, but feel free to go out to the stables. In the morning, though, I expect to see you both out in the ring by nine sharp."

Jill waved her hand airily. "Why so late? We'll be out by eight at the latest."

He laughed. "We'll see about that. I know what a bedbug you are. By the way, Cara's planning dinner for about seven o'clock, if that's not too late for you ladies."

"I brought along some chips in my suitcase, Uncle Alex," Jill said, teasing, "just to ford off starvation."

"Good." He winked. "Then I'll see you later."

"Cara?" Maura looked quizzically at Jill after her uncle left.

"The housekeeper."

Maura nodded. "I like your aunt and uncle."

"Nice people."

"I can't wait to get out to the stables."

"Get unpacking, buddy. Gosh, I don't believe I brought along so much stuff!"

"Me either." Maura giggled. "And why in heaven's name I packed this long dress I'll never know. Where am I going to wear it?"

"Oh, we'll have several balls, m'lady." Jill winked. "I told you—this is going to be your summer for boys!"

Within half an hour, their clothes thrown more or less neatly into drawers and closets, the girls were crossing the gravel toward the barns. "I can't wait to show you Barnabas, my favorite bay gelding," Jill said. "Uncle Alex keeps telling me I've spoiled him and practically turned him into a house pet, but he's such a sweetheart. We'll find a special horse for you, too, other than the regular hacks Uncle Alex lets out to his students."

"He gives lessons?" I thought this was a breeding farm."

"It is, but he enjoys teaching when he has the time."

Maura's eyes were alight as they passed stall after stall of beautiful horses. They paused first besides Barnabas, and Maura looked on as Jill renewed her friendship with the gelding, feeding him some sugar cubes and part of an apple. Then they moved on to the other barn where the Warren-bred hunters were kept. Jill pointed out one mare in particular—a sleek, ebony-coated five-year-old named Blackfire. For Maura it was love at first sight, but any hopes Maura had of trying her out were dashed when Jill said she was her uncle's prize, a treasure he'd trained himself and for whom he had high hopes. Still, they remained by the stall for several minutes as Maura stroked the mare's silky nose and dreamed of what it would be like to be up on her back.

10

Jill led the way out of the barn to the riding rings. Beyond lay the pastures, which lifted gradually to the hills in the distance.

"We'll take a ride up there tomorrow or the next day," Jill said, waving her hand. "There're lots of nice trails through the woods and over the hills. And tomorrow afternoon I thought I'd take you down to the club for swimming or a couple of sets of tennis—you brought your racket, didn't you?"

"I did."

"My old friends should all be at the club. You'll get to meet them."

As the two girls sat on the split-rail fence chatting and watching the horses in the field, Maura was considering her first impressions of the farm, anticipating what was in store in the days ahead. Already she was infatuated with the rolling, emerald landscape, the horses and stables, the Warrens' warm friendliness. She wondered if Jill realized how fortunate she was to have been able to spend her summers here year after year. For Maura the novelty of being on her own, out from under her parents' protective wings for the first time in her life was exhilarating. Not that her parents had ever thought of anything other than her happiness, but there were times when their overflowing love seemed almost suffocating. This summer she would be able to make decisions for herself, and she was really looking forward to it.

Gradually the sun dipped out of sight behind the hills and it was time to go in to get ready for dinner.

Since it was the girls' first night, the meal was served in the formal dining room with its lush oriental carpet and fine antique furnishings. As they filled their plates with vegetables, potatoes, and thin slices of roast beef, Lorna Warren smiled. "So, how did your first afternoon go? Have you given Maura the grand tour?"

"An abbreviated version. We went through the stables, of course."

"I would never have guessed." Lorna chuckled. "Did you choose a mount, Maura?"

"I thought I'd leave that to Mr. Warren. But the mare, Blackfire, really impressed me. What a beauty! Who does the training?"

"Oh, we try to share the responsibilities. Alex does the initial breaking, then turns the green hunters over to me for schooling. It works out rather well."

"By the way, girls," Alex interrupted, "I believe I have a pleasant surprise for you. Jill, you remember the end-of-summer show that's usually held at the Birchwood Hunt Club?"

"How could I forget? It's one of the best shows in New England."

"Well, it's going to be held here this year." He tried to keep his voice blasé but wasn't entirely successful.

"Here! Uncle Alex, you must be kidding. That's absolutely fantastic! How'd you manage it, Uncle Alex?"

"A bit of finagling here and there."

"You must be thrilled."

"That's an understatement." Lorna laughed. "Your uncle has yet to come down to earth."

"Now, Lorna, you know you're as excited as I am. But what I was wondering," he continued mildly, "was whether you girls would like to try your luck?"

Jill and Maura stared at him.

"I'm quite serious."

"But how could we?" Jill exclaimed. "We're not professionals."

"It will be a two-day meet with a variety of classes, novice to expert, and you'll have plenty of opportunity to train during the next month and a half."

"I don't know about myself, Uncle Alex," Jill hesitated. "Maybe in one of the novice classes, but Maura's great."

Maura was startled as everyone turned and looked at her expectantly. "Wait a minute." She shook her head quickly. "Jill's exaggerating."

"You've always been too modest," Jill said. "With enough practice you could compete against the best of them."

"Jill, please..."

"Please what? I know you too well. You can't tell me that deep down inside you wouldn't like to give it a try."

"Yes, I would. But I've never ridden against professionals before. I might make a fool of myself."

"You wouldn't."

"Well," Alex interrupted, "no need for a decision tonight. You can show me your stuff

13

tomorrow morning in the ring. Let's put the subject on hold till then."

Chapter 2

Maura was up at daybreak. She looked over at Jill, still sound asleep, but Maura was too excited to sleep any longer. Already she was picturing herself on a sleek hunter at the upcoming show, taking the fences to a round of applause, trotting to the judges' stand to collect her blue ribbon. Was it a silly daydream, she wondered, or could she really do it? Mentally she checked off her positive points—good seat, good hands, a natural sense of timing—but she'd never attempted anything beyond the amateur shows at the riding club at home.

Moving quietly so as not to waken Jill, Maura put on her slippers and robe and went across the hall to the bathroom to shower. She was already dressing in riding boots and chaps when Jill groggily sat up in bed.

"What time is it? You shouldn't have let me sleep so late."

"Relax, it's only seven. I couldn't sleep."

"Not excited or anything, are you?" Jill teased as she ran her fingers through her tousled hair. "Throw me my robe, will you, Maura? I don't even begin to wake up 'til I'm in the shower. Don't wait for me—go on downstairs if you want. Aunt Lorna's up early, and Cara probably has a pot of coffee on." She stuffed her arms into the sleeves of her robe and searched beside the bed for her slippers.

"Okay, see you in the kitchen."

"Mmm," Jill mumbled.

The scent of fresh-perked coffee greeted Maura as she descended the stairs toward the kitchen. Sure enough, Lorna was at the table. She smiled as Maura entered. "Well, good morning. Another early bird. Jill's not up yet, is she?"

"She's in the shower."

"Maura, you must be a miracle worker. Generally Jill has to be prodded several times." She laughed. "Would you like some coffee? Or do you prefer tea or milk?"

"Coffee's fine."

"Have a seat." Lorna turned to face the cheerfully plump woman who was already approaching the table with a cup in hand. "Cara, I don't believe you've met Jill's friend, Maura. Maura, this is Cara White, our housekeeper. Without her help this old house would be a shambles."

"Nice to meet you, Cara." Maura smiled.

"And you, too, miss. Good to see Jill's got some company up for the summer. I've got some bacon and eggs almost ready on the stove, or can I get you something else?"

"Bacon and eggs, thanks. I'll be needing energy today."

15

"Perfect weather for riding," Mrs. Warren remarked, "clear and cool enough so that the animals won't be sluggish. I'll be doing some schooling this morning. With this show coming up, there's so much to be done."

"Will you be competing?"

"Yes, in one of the hunter classes. I have a special gelding I'm dying to try out."

As Maura stirred her coffee, she heard a jovial baritone voice behind her. "Good morning, ladies. Ready to ride, Maura?"

"Sure am."

"You can have Snappers this morning—a nice jumper and easy handler." He paused beside the table to give his wife a peck on the cheek.

Cara returned with three steaming plates of food. "Morning, Mr. Warren. You're just in time."

"I know. I waited for the smell of frying bacon to lure me downstairs. Jill up yet?"

"I'm here, Uncle Alex. Heavens, it's not even eight o'clock. What are my eyes doing open?" She kissed her aunt, then her uncle. "I'm starving. Bacon and eggs. Thanks, Cara, just the way I like them."

"I've told Maura to take Snapper this morning," Alex said after Jill took her place at the table.

"Oh, you'll like him, Maura. You riding, Uncle Alex?"

"Not today. I think I'll spend the morning watching you two. Later, I have to go into town,

16

and this afternoon I've got to give two private lessons."

"You're giving a lot of lessons this year," Jill noted.

"More than usual, but I enjoy it."

There was silence at the table as everyone concentrated on breakfast. Maura and Jill finished first and excused themselves.

Alex waved them off. "I'll meet you in the ring in a few minutes. Get your horses out and tacked up."

One of the men hired full-time to groom and care for the horses was just opening the barn doors as Maura and Jill approached. He looked up as Jill called out. "Hi there, Charlie. How are you?"

"Just fine, just fine," the lean, gray-haired man answered. "Up for the summer again, are you?"

"Sure am. Charlie, this is my girlfriend, Maura Langdon. She'll be spending the summer with me."

"Pleased to meet you," he said extending a calloused hand. His grip was firm and strong. "Riding this morning, girls?"

"Yes, Barnabas and Snappers."

"Go get your tack, and I'll lead them out for you."

"Thanks, Charlie. This way, Maura." Jill strode off down the center aisle of the barn toward the tack room. Pushing open the door, she went to the far wall, where rows of bridles and martingales were hanging on wooden pegs.

"This is Snappers', I think...Yes, here's her name. Catch." She tossed the gear to Maura. "The saddles are over there. Take the one on the end. And here's mine. Ready?"

They returned to the main part of the barn, where the horses were standing in crossties. Charlie gave them a wave of his hand and resumed feeding and watering the rest of the horses.

As they came to the chestnut in the first set of crossties, Jill motioned. "Snappers. He's real easygoing. You shouldn't have any trouble tacking him up." The horse rolled his eyes back in his head, watching their progress. Maura lifted a soothing hand to his neck.

"Hi, there, boy. Pleased to meet you. I think we'll be friends and have a good ride today."

The gelding's ears flickered at the sound of Maura's voice. He snorted, then nickered as she continued to pat his neck.

"I'll go tend to that dark fellow up there," Jill added.

Maura pulled a sugar cube from her pocket and fed it palm up to the now acquiescent Snappers. Then she slipped the saddle with its attached sheep's fleece blanket onto his back and buckled the girth. He was still crunching his sugar cube. Slipping the halter from his head, she brought up the bridle, and he took the bit without a hint of resistance. Finally, Maura brought the leather pieces up over his ears and tightened the chin strap.

"Ready to go, my man?"

18

Jill walked by with Barnabas. "All set?"

They waited to mount until they were in the ring. Once in the saddle, Maura adjusted her stirrups. She had just started Snappers at a walk along the fence to loosen his muscles when Alex Warren arrived.

"That's it. Walk them around a bit. Two laps then a posting trot."

Snappers handled beautifully. Not an excessively spirited animal, he was nevertheless smooth gaited and quick to respond. When she'd circled the ring a few times at trot, Maura heard Alex Warren's call. "Let's get their blood pumping. Put them into a canter."

At the touch of Maura's heel, Snappers sprang forward on the right lead, as exhilarated as Maura by the morning romp. A few moments later, Maura heard Alex Warren again. "Figure eights at a canter."

Maura began, turning Snappers in from the rail toward the center of the ring and stopping him smoothly at dead center. Then, with a touch of her heel, she immediately put him into a canter again on the opposite lead. She headed out again toward the rail, completed the top loop of the eight, swung back toward the center, stopped and repeated the procedure.

"Good . . . excellent," Alex called. "Jill, your turn."

Jill stumbled through her first eight. "You're not stopping him completely in the canter," her uncle noted. "He's getting off on the wrong lead. Again. Okay . . . yes . . . better."

Alex hopped down from his seat on the fence. "Let's try some jumps. Begin with the X. Maura, you first."

Maura headed Snappers toward the X at a trot, then lifted into a half seat, her head up, her eyes forward. Just before the crossed rails, she squeezed with her legs. Snappers skimmed over the low jump, landed, and moved away at a canter.

Jill followed suit.

"Good. Now the X and the rail."

The girls continued until they were up to four fences. At that point Alex Warren stopped them. "Walk them a while, and we'll try a course." He strode across the ring and adjusted the height of the rails and the angle of the gate. "Okay, girls, now pay attention. Here's the course." He motioned with his hands as he spoke. "First the in and out, then down the rail, around the brush, cross over to the red gate, the rail, then around to the barrels, the wall, and the white gate. Jill, you first."

"Oh, Uncle Alex..."

"Come on, you can do it. The wall's the hardest, and you've taken that before."

"Okay, but I'll probably end up on my head."

She headed Barnabas toward the in and out—three fences, each successively higher, the distance of a horse's stride between them—at a trot and went through it neatly. Although she completed the rest of the course in less than perfect form, at least she stayed in the saddle.

"See, I told you." Jill shook her head

disgustedly as she returned to where her uncle and Maura were waiting.

"Nothing a little practicing and polishing won't correct. Okay, Maura."

Maura felt confident as she began. This was what she loved—the challenge of the open course before her. As she and Snappers sailed through the in and out, Maura's eyes were already riveted on the next jump, gauging the distance. A slight pressure of her hands on the reins checked the horse's stride when they landed, and they moved off at a canter toward the rail. The jump was clean and perfectly timed, but Maura's mind was concentrated only on what lay ahead.

Clearing the brush with inches to spare, Maura turned Snappers up the center of the ring. His stride never faltered as they approached the red gate. Maura then squeezed her legs at precisely the right moment, and they were up, over, and landing. Three strides to the next jump, over it, into a right-lead canter and around to the last three, most difficult jumps of the course. With a long leap, Snappers cleared the barrels, Maura collected him in preparation for the higher wall, utilizing the gelding's full power as they flew over the obstacle successfully. Then they went on and finished with the white gate. Only as they were cantering back toward the top of the ring did Maura allow herself to relax, dropping her hand to pat the horse's damp neck. "Good boy... nice job!"

21

The wide grins on Jill and Alex's faces were an indication of her performance. Alex wasted no words. "My girl, I'm impressed. You're a natural... have all the makings of a fine open jumper. Now don't let the praise go to your head—there's still a lot of work ahead if you're to take the ribbon at the show, but I think we should give it a try. Agreed?"

"Oh, yes... yes, and thank you!"

"From now on, you have a standing appointment with me at nine every morning. You'll need another mount, too. Snappers is a good all-around hunter, but he hasn't the makings to compete in the big time. I think we'll begin training you on Blackfire."

"Blackfire!" Maura gasped. "Mr. Warren, I don't know how to thank you!"

"No thanks are necessary. I'm not being purely unselfish, you know. I've been waiting for an opportunity to show Blackfire, but I've never found the right rider to do it. After what I've seen this morning, I believe you're the girl I've been looking for."

"I hope I don't let you down."

Alex Warren laughed. "You won't. I wouldn't suggest this if I thought otherwise. Well, I think we've given these gentlemen enough of a workout for one morning. Cool them out and bring them back to the barn. I've got to get into town. See you later." Waving his hand, he strode off toward his car.

After he had gone, Maura turned excitedly to Jill. "I don't believe it! He seems to think I have a chance."

"You *do,* silly. I told you that from the beginning."

"Your uncle didn't say what class I'd be entering. One of the hunter divisions, I imagine."

Jill chuckled. "Don't bet on it. If I know my uncle, he'll be aiming for the top—open jumping."

While Maura absorbed that bit of information, Jill began to dismount. "Come on. If we're going to cool out these horses, we'd better get off their backs and start walking them."

Chapter 3

Early that afternoon the girls set off in Jill's sports car for the private club at the other side of the village. In a valley between rolling green hills were a golf course, several tennis courts, a pool area, and a small lake. Jill pulled into the narrow paved road that led down to the pool and courts, then parked near the converted farmhouse that now served as a clubhouse.

Not surprisingly, the parking lot was crowded, as was the pool area, and there was a waiting line for the tennis courts. As the girls left the car and walked toward the pool, Jill scrutinized the crowd.

"See anyone you know?" Maura questioned.

"Over at the end of the pool...Liz Brooks and Allison Reilly. Those boys they're with look vaguely familiar, too."

Maura glanced toward the tall redhead and shorter brunette sitting on lounge chairs chatting to each other. The redhead spotted Jill, waved, and called out. "Jill, is that you?"

"Sure is. Hi, Liz."

"Hey, good to see you again. You can always tell it's summer when you show up."

"Liz, Allison, this is Maura Langdon, my cohort at Maryvale. Maura, the girls."

"Nice to meet you, Maura. Jill, you remember Jeff Gates and Larry Corbette, don't you?"

"Yes. Hi, guys."

Maura nodded, then turned away quickly. She remembered Jill's pledge to introduce her to boys, and once again a feeling of shyness overwhelmed her. The feeling grew worse when she noticed Jeff and Larry's appreciative gazes as she slipped out of her beach robe, revealing her graceful figure in a white, two-piece suit.

"Want to take a swim," Jill asked, "or catch some sun?"

"Let's swim," Maura mumbled, anxious to get away from those watchful eyes.

"My sentiments exactly. It's getting warm."

As Maura started toward the pool's edge, Jill called back to the others. "Be back in a minute. "We're going to try the water."

The girls dove cleanly into the water, surfaced, then swam to the far side of the pool in smooth strokes. After pausing for a moment to catch their breath, they pushed off again, swimming side by side for several laps, alternating back and breast strokes, until, out of breath but laughing, they heaved themselves out of the water.

After squeezing the excess moisture from her long hair, Maura found her towel and spread it out on the cement bordering the pool. Jill plopped down beside her.

"The way you two match strokes," Liz Reilly remarked, "you could put on a show."

"We practice together in the swim club at school," explained Jill, "though I never realized we were *that* good."

"Don't let it go to your head. You're not," Allison kidded. "So when did you two come up?"

"Yesterday. As soon as classes were over for the year, we packed our bags and headed north. Maura's going to be spending the whole summer with me at the farm."

Maura lay back on her towel, content to listen as the girls continued their conversation. Closing her eyes, she relished the warmth of the sun beating down on her face and body. When the heat and the buzz of voices in the background, she let her thoughts drift, until Jill's loud voice roused her.

"Hi there, Bill. Come over and join us. Maura." Jill tapped her shoulder. "Come back to the living. Here's someone I want you to meet."

Maura sat up, resting her weight on her elbows.

"This is Bill Peters, Maura, an old friend of mine. We've been palling around every summer since I was a kid. Bill, Maura Langdon, my best friend."

Maura looked up to see a tall, sun-bronzed blond staring down at her. He squatted near her towel, his blue eyes twinkling as he smiled. "Hello, Maura. So, I'm finally meeting Jill's gorgeous friend. She's told me a lot about you."

Maura blushed. Handling flattery wasn't one of her strong points. She tried unsuccessfully to relax under his scrutiny and wished she had the same ease of conversation with strangers, especially boy strangers, as Jill. Knowing some response on her part was necessary, she tried to think of some lighthearted reply but couldn't.

Still, Bill continued, "You're spending the summer in Southbury?"

"Yes I'm looking forward to it," Maura said, looking down at the cement, feeling flustered and awkward.

"Great area. I've lived here all my life, and I love it. What do you girls have planned?"

"Lots," Jill bubbled. "Uncle Alex already has Maura training for the show at the end of the summer."

"You're a good rider then."

"I try," she said softly.

"From what I understand, it's going to be quite a show. Mr. Warren was talking to me about it the other day. My parents' place is two doors down," he clarified.

26

"Do you ride?" Maura asked.

"Poorly. Not that I don't admire the skill in someone else. I have better luck with sailing. I'll be taking my sunfish out on the lake this afternoon, as a matter of fact. I'd invite you two along for a ride, but I only have room for one passenger."

"Thanks, anyway," Maura smiled. There was a moment's silence as Maura twisted her sunglasses nervously in her hands.

"You're in Jill's class, right? So I guess you have another year at Maryvale."

Maura nodded.

"And then what are your plans?"

"I'll probably go into music."

He studied her face until Maura felt a flush rising in her cheeks. "Feel like a swim?" he asked abruptly.

"Sure," Maura said, though she wasn't at all sure she wanted to. "Jill?" she asked.

"Thanks, but I think I'll catch a few more rays. You two go ahead."

Maura wanted to glare at her friend for leaving her on her own like this, but Jill's eyes were closed. Before Maura could change her mind, Bill reached down for her hand and helped her up.

As they swam, treaded water, talked, and swam some more, Maura began to relax. Bill was really a nice guy, pleasant, talkative, with a good sense of humor. By the time they climbed out to lie on beach towels beside Jill, Maura felt perfectly comfortable. Her nervousness was gone.

"You're a good swimmer," she told him.

"Likewise, but I've always enjoyed any kind of athletics—horseback riding excluded." He chuckled. "I'll be going to Boston University in the fall, and I hope to make their ski team this year. Do you ski?"

"The cold and I don't get along too well together. Jill's the pro in that department."

Bill cocked an inquisitive brow in Jill's direction. "Really? Since I only see her in the hot and sunny weather, I never would have guessed."

"I'll just have to invite myself up for the Christmas holidays then." Jill grinned, full of mischief. "You can take me out on the slopes and discover my hidden talents."

He laughed and tweaked her nose teasingly.

The rest of the afternoon passed quickly. Maura couldn't believe it when Jill looked at her watch and announced it was after five. "We'd better get going, or Aunt Lorna will send out a search party."

Bill smiled as Jill and Maura said their goodbyes. "I'll have just enough time for a short sail. It's been a fun afternoon. We'll see each other again soon, I hope." His eyes caught Maura's and held them until, in confusion, she looked away. "Take care, Jill."

"You, too, Bill. Stop over at the farm and say hello."

"I'll do that."

As Jill headed her MG out of the parking lot, she grinned at Maura. "Nice, isn't he?"

"I suppose. What are you up to, anyway? A little matchmaking?"

"Who, me?" Jill exclaimed. "Not really. This was just to break the ice."

Maura had to smile at the intuitiveness of her friend. Although she had enjoyed meeting Bill, any thought of romance was far from her mind. Maura had never really given any serious thought to boys, and certainly she had never experienced the yearnings and heart palpitations that so many of her friends described to her. She'd be just as happy to live in a world without them; she didn't feel she was missing anything.

Chapter 4

Maura's first lesson the next morning went well. Blackfire handled as beautifully as she looked. Longlegged for a mare, she stood sixteen hands, and despite her strong hindquarters, her every line was classic grace, her every move a study of perfection. Maura and the mare immediately formed a unique partnership—a bond between an animal and human who both loved what they were doing and strived to do their best.

After lunch Jill and Maura saddled up again

for a ride across the Warrens' pastures and up into the hills. Maura had chosen to ride Snappers, since she knew he performed well on the rough woodland trails.

Cantering across the meadows, then slowing to a walk as they picked their way along the meandering path under the trees, the girls had been out for almost an hour when they paused at a clearing high up on the hillside. Maura sighed as she looked at the beautiful panorama before her. Low, rolling mountains with verdant valleys between, velvet green pastures, stone walls and old colonial homes. It was a perfect picture of the beauty of New England.

As they started out again, Jill pointed to a tumbling stone wall on their right. "Want to follow it?" she asked Maura.

"Where does it go?"

"Don't know. Let's check it out."

"As long as you can find our way back."

The wall led them through the woods and over the crest of the hill, where the trees gave way to a wide expanse of open land. In the distance, where the land sloped down toward the valley, stood a large brick house its red tones mellowed by age. Surrounding it were lawns, formal gardens, white-fenced paddocks, a stable, and barn.

"Wow," exclaimed Jill.

"Who owns it?"

"I don't know. I never realized it was here, but what a place. Horse people, too, from the looks of it."

Continuing along the fence until the house was out of sight, the girls passed through another woods before arriving at a fair-sized natural meadow that was secluded from the rest of the landscape by a ring of trees. In its center, where the land dipped into a hollow, the waters of a willow-draped pond glimmered in the sunlight.

"This is gorgeous," Jill exclaimed as she heeled her horse forward.

"We'd better go back, Jill," Maura cautioned. "I think we might be trespassing."

"Oh, come on, worrywart," Jill scoffed. "There's no one around, and we're not disturbing anything."

"I don't know. Look over there," Maura said quietly.

Both girls were silent as they stared at the horseman cantering toward them from the opposite side of the meadow. Even from the distance, it was clear he was an expert rider and that the horse he was riding was a thoroughbred.

Maura was unable to draw her eyes away from the broad-shouldered figure who drew up beside them. Looking a couple of years older than herself, this handsome, tall, dark-haired boy with black-lashed green eyes looked self-assured, poised, and confident.

The three studied each other carefully. The boy's eyes glanced over them both but paused on Maura. Feeling his gaze, she felt uneasy and wished they'd turned back earlier.

31

"I don't know if you're aware," he said, his deep voice finally shattering the stillness, "but this is private property."

For a change Jill was silent, nearly gaping at the dark-haired stranger. It was up to Maura to say something and, feeling oddly shaken by his appearance, she couldn't seem to pull her gaze from his face. "Sorry," she said somewhat distractedly. "We must have ridden further than we thought."

Finding her voice at last, Jill said hurriedly, "Yeah, we just came over from my uncle's farm over the hill. I'm Jill Warren, and this is Maura Langdon."

The boy acknowledged Jill only briefly. "I thought you seemed familiar. I don't believe we've met, though I know your aunt and uncle. They're quite good friends of my parents. Kevin DeAngelo," he curtly introduced himself.

"I remember hearing the name," Jill said. "Your family owns Maple Park."

"You're standing on a part of it now," he reminded her.

"And the house and barns we saw back there in the distance?"

He nodded.

"I've never ridden this far up the mountain, and I guess I lost track of my uncle's property lines."

He was silent. His eyes had already returned to Maura. There was something about the way he looked at her that upset her. It was as if he were trying to read her thoughts. In her discomfort she spoke quickly, her eyes fixed on

Jill. "We'd better go—we have a long ride back." She started to turn Snappers when Kevin DeAngelo's voice stopped her.

"You're staying with the Warrens?" he asked, still staring intently at her.

"Yes. For the summer," she answered quickly, anxious to get away.

"Are you planning on riding in the show?"

She could see that getting away wouldn't be so easy. Still, his question surprised her. Why would he be interested?

"Well, yes, as a matter of fact, I am," she answered directly.

"Which class?"

"It's not definite, probably open jumping."

His bows raised a fraction. "Hmmm, stiff competition."

"I know."

"Maybe I'll see you around this summer."

"Perhaps," Maura said briefly. What was it about him that both attracted and infuriated her? It was true that he was strikingly good-looking, but there was an air of superiority in his carriage and voice that she found very irritating. Yet she knew that he was causing emotions to stir within her that she had never known existed.

"We'll be down at the club for tennis and swimming," Jill interjected in her friendly way.

"Will you?" His indifferent tone, implying that it was of no concern to him where they went, startled Jill.

"Well! Sorry again for trespassing," Jill said haughtily.

33

"I suppose you can find your way back." he said, his tone mocking.

"We'll manage." Maura couldn't stop the cold edge that slipped into her voice. How dare he be so rude to Jill, who'd never said a cruel word to anyone in her life! She was furious.

"Goodbye, then." Without waiting for their reply, he swung around and cantered off.

Jill shook her head at the retreating figure. "Isn't *he* something! I can't believe I've never met him, but then I've heard the DeAngelos travel a lot in the summer. Handsome, though! What did you think?"

"I thought he was a conceited snob," Maura spat out. "How you can say *anything* nice about him after he was so rude, I don't understand!"

"Well, you may not have noticed, Miss Horse-woman, but he was really giving you the eye the whole time."

"Was he?" To her chagrin Maura found her own eyes were following the broad-shouldered back moving off into the distance.

"Come on, you must have noticed—though he's probably used to girls falling at his feet."

"Well, *I* have no intention of ever doing so!" Maura was amazed at her own vehemence. Then she said more thoughtfully, "I wonder if he's riding in the show?"

"If he wasn't, he wouldn't have been so interested in finding out if *you* were, though we can check when we get home. Uncle Alex has a list of all the entries to date."

That evening they asked Alex about Kevin

DeAngelo. Alex didn't need to check his records to give them an answer. Kevin DeAngelo was definitely planning to compete in the show—in open jumping.

Chapter 5

Every day Maura was up with the birds, charged with energy and ready for her lessons. Although Alex Warren didn't dare compliment her too fully for fear she would grow lax in the spotlight of praise, Maura knew he was extremely pleased with her progress. On many occasions her lessons continued well beyond the scheduled hour.

Sometimes people came to the rails of the ring to watch her practice but Maura, concentrating on her riding, was never aware of them until the lesson was over. One morning Bill Peters stopped by. She saw him coming up the drive as she led Blackfire into the ring, but she was too preoccupied to acknowledge him. Alex Warren was already waiting for her, and he gave her a leg up into the saddle, then checked the girth.

"Alright, Maura, the usual warm-up. Walk

her a few minutes to loosen her muscles, two rounds at a trot, two at a canter, and we'll get into the jumping."

Blackfire shook her head in anticipation as Maura loosened the tension on the reins and headed her off at a walk along the railing. As Maura passed Alex in her first swing at a posting trot, he called out, "Half seat!" Maura dropped her heels, lifted herself slightly out of the saddle, her back arched, her shoulders straight. "Get those heels down! I don't want to see your hands on her neck. It's all in the legs. Pull in your knees! Okay, good. Sitting trot . . . walk . . . now canter—one round sitting, one round hunt seat."

"Okay, good," he continued when she had finished and come to a halt beside him. "Twice over the X, then the X and the rail, I want to work on gymnastics today and the wall."

As Maura warmed up Blackfire on the X, Alex strode over to the far side of the ring where five fences were set up in succession, beginning with an X and ending with a three-foot rail. He paced out the distance between each fence, checking their placement carefully, then turned as Maura finished her second X and cross-rail.

"She should be primed by now. Start her in to the fences . . . posting trot almost to the X or she'll get too excited and rush. Good."

Maura knew the rhythm perfectly. With a horse's stride between each fence, it was land, squeeze hard with her legs, up, over, land, squeeze, up, over, down the line, each fence a bit higher, until they were through and cantering away.

Mr. Warren went to the first fence, removed the X, and dropped the rail into the first notch, then went back to the last fence and raised its rail six inches. "This time at a canter." As Maura approached he barked, "Keep her collected—she's rushing!" When Maura was a few yards from the first fence, he cried, "Hunt seat now!" Blackfire lifted into the air, landed. "Squeeze...squeeze...squeeze...squeeze!"

Maura cleared the last fence, cantered off, circled Blackfire back, and brought her down to a trot. Alex Warren was raising the last fence again.

"I'm bringing it up to four feet, Maura. You're really going to have to squeeze after the fourth fence. She's still rushing a bit. I guess you can sense it."

"Yes," Maura agreed. "She gets too excited."

"Try sitting the canter right up to the first fence. It will be more difficult, and you're going to have to move fast into your hunt seat."

"I can manage."

"I want to see your head and eyes well up and facing ahead. If you drop your eyes one fraction before that last fence, she'll hesitate—and disaster."

"Gotcha."

"Then go to it."

Trying to keep Blackfire as calm as possible, Maura walked her across to the opposite rail. Still, the mare knew what was coming and jumped right into her canter when given the signal. As they came around the end of the ring, Maura maintained a firm tension on the reins and sank her heels even deeper into the stirrups until the muscles pulled in the backs of her calves. They were approaching smoothly this time; Blackfire's stride was checked and collected. At the last moment before the fence, Maura lifted into a hunt seat, squeezed her legs into Blackfire's sides, and the rhythm began—up, over, land, squeeze. Maura kept her eyes well up, focusing on the branches of a tree in the distance. When she got to the last fence, Maura felt Blackfire coming up beneath her, soaring, flying.

"Excellent," Alex Warren called. "Perfect timing. The last fence was magnificent. You cleared it with a good six inches to spare. Walk her a minute, then on to the wall."

The wall was a plywood creation built and painted to resemble a stone wall. It was about three feet high, two feet wide, and eight feet long, and had taller posts at each end into which rails could be set to raise the height of the jump and increase the difficulty.

Still elated from her success at the gymnastics, Maura headed Blackfire toward the wall. Eyes up, she timed her paces. She'd need a strong jump and early take off. When Maura knew the moment was right, she squeezed. Blackfire lifted, was over, landed, then almost stumbled.

Alex Warren shouted from behind. "Release, Maura! You didn't release! How can you expect that angel to fly over a fence with her chin tucked against her neck! Again! And think what you're doing!"

"Sorry... sorry," Maura mumbled as she turned Blackfire for another approach. This time her mind was totally on her riding, and she could hear Alex Warren shouting, "Release!" as Blackfire lifted off, Maura didn't need the reminder as she moved the reins up the mare's neck, giving her room to stretch her graceful form.

"All right... better. This time I want you to stop her four strides from the jump, turn, and approach from the opposite direction. Go."

It wasn't an easy task stopping Blackfire once she was moving. As Maura leaned back in the saddle, the mare fought the pressure of the reins, shaking her elegant head.

"Stop her! Okay, now turn, organize yourself, and canter."

The second time through, Blackfire realized what was expected of her, and Maura's life was made a lot simpler.

"Walk her while I raise the jump."

Blackfire was working up a sweat, as was Maura, who could feel droplets of perspiration on her forehead and between her shoulder blades. Alex settled the rail in place over the wall, strode to the side, and motioned Maura to circle round and begin to canter.

"That's it, keep her steady... steady... now squeeze! Release! Stop her! Okay. Once again. You're forcing her to use that power when she needs it, and that's what I want to see. This time continue down over the gate and the brush."

Maura did as he instructed, clearing the wall neatly and in perfect form. But she was tiring. As they approached the brush, she let her legs relax for just one instant—just long enough to throw Blackfire off. They took the brush disjointedly as the mare jumped without clear direction. Maura shook her head disgustedly as she pulled the mare down into a trot.

"Sloppy, Maura! That last fence was terrible! She had control, and you were a sack of potatoes along for the ride."

"I know...I know. I'm sorry," Maura said wearily, "but I'm tired."

"Tired! Is that an excuse? Do you want a blue ribbon in that show, or don't you?"

"Yes, yes."

"Then erase any thoughts of tiredness from your mind. Again! All three fences...with style this time, and keep those knees tight!"

"Yes, sir." Maura sighed and took several deep breaths to give herself a new reserve of energy. Hurt and embarrassed by Alex Warren's criticism, she headed Blackfire toward the wall with new determination. As though the mare sensed her rider's state of mind, she shook her elegant head, snorted, put greater power into her stride, and cleared the wall in a superb leap. Maura's total concentration was on the fences ahead. She forced her heels further down and pulled her knees in. Her head up, her legs tight, she was one with the horse beneath her as they cantered and soared, cantered and soared.

40

"Bravo! Now that's the way I want you to ride *all* the time! Keep it up and the blue ribbon is ours!" He was all smiles, and was quick to pat Blackfire's damp neck. "You both deserve a rest after that performance. Cool her out, and see that Charlie sponges her down before she's put away. Come on down. I'll take the saddle now, and she'll cool that much faster." He steadied the mare as Maura threw her leg over and dismounted. "I'll bet you feel it in your legs this morning." He grinned.

"They're like rubber bands."

He laughed. "The walk should do you some good then, too." In a moment he had the saddle off Blackfire's lathered back and was walking beside Maura to the gate. "Take her in the shade and let her nibble on the lawn."

As she left the ring with Blackfire, several riders waiting to enter called out to her, "Good ride."

"Thanks . . . thanks a lot." She smiled and saw Bill Peters approaching. "Hi, there. I saw you come up when I started my lesson, but I didn't think you'd still be here."

He fell into step beside her as she headed across to the lawn. "And why shouldn't I be? I'm impressed."

Maura laughed self-consciously. "If you've been here the whole time, you must have seen and heard that I did plenty wrong, too."

"Put me in that ring, and you'd see a lot more things done wrong. Poor Alex would throw up his hands in disgust."

Maura smiled. "You can't be *that* bad."

41

"Oh, yes, I could. Horsemanship is definitely not one of my greater talents."

"I have to walk her for a while," Maura patted the mare's neck.

"I'll walk along with you, if you don't mind."

"Not at all."

The two stepped into the welcome shade of the trees just as Lorna appeared at the back door holding two cans of soda. "I thought you might need a refresher," she called out.

"Sure do," Maura answered. "Thanks."

Jogging over to take the sodas from Mrs. Warren, Bill popped the tops and handed a can to Maura, who took a long swallow. "Oh, that tastes good. My mouth felt like cotton."

"After all that exercise, I'm not surprised."

They talked easily as they strolled along, pausing now and then to let Blackfire eat grass.

"Do you get to do much riding at school?"

"None at all—no stables. My mother comes up twice a week to take me to the riding club, but that's it."

"Gee, that's a shame. At least I've been able to take advantage of all the organized sports I want—though that may change this year. I'm going to have to spend more time with the books."

"What are you majoring in?"

"Pre-law."

"Pretty impressive."

"Yep, it's what I've wanted to do ever since I can remember, and all the studying will be worth it. This town needs a good attorney. Too many people have to travel all the way to Danbury for good legal advice."

"Good luck."

"And you, too. You said you were interested in music?"

"Yes, though I don't know what I'm going to do with it."

"What do you play?"

"Piano, mostly, and a little bit of flute."

"Maybe I'll get to hear you play," Bill said.

"I doubt it. I haven't been able to practice at all since I've been here. I must be rusty." Maura reached out a hand to Blackfire's flank and found her fairly cool.

"You'll want to get her stabled," Bill remarked. "And I'd better be going—I've got some things to do. Maybe I'll see you later."

"Fine. That would be fun. And thanks for walking with me. Take care."

"You, too."

He sauntered off, turning once to lift his hand in a wave.

When Maura brought Blackfire to the barn for her sponging, she found Jill hanging over Barnabas's stall, feeding him bits of carrots. Her eyes twinkled with mischief as she spied Maura.

"You and Bill had a nice walk, I see. I've never known him to show such an interest in horses before."

"Oh, can it, Jill." Maura grinned. "He was just being friendly."

"You noticed how well I kept myself out of the way?"

43

"You're trying to fix us up, right?" Maura loosened Blackfire's bridle and reached for her halter.

"No," Jill mused, "honestly I'm not. Bill's not your type. I have someone else in mind for you."

"Oh? Who?"

"My secret. You'll find out soon enough. And I have my own plans for Bill."

As Maura hooked the mare into the cross-ties, she threw Jill a sly look. "I *thought* you liked him! So why are you pushing the two of us together? You must be crazy!"

"Far from it. I figured I'd let him get you out of his system. Look, you're pretty and so-phisticated; he's good-looking, athletic—you two were bound to be attracted to each other. But I knew the sooner you had a chance to talk and be together, the sooner you'd realize you weren't cut from the same mold."

"And where do you, Madame Psychologist, come into all of this?"

"Mid to end summer, when you're up to your ears in your riding and Bill needs a little friendly companionship. Who else will he come to but his old buddy two houses down the road? I've always been good for a cheerful word and a laugh."

"There's a lot more to you than that," Maura stated, "and you know it."

"Of course I do. But he doesn't—yet. I intend for him to find out this summer."

Maura shook her head in bemusement. She was relieved, at least, that Jill had given up her efforts at pairing her with Bill. But who was this other person Jill had in mind? Aside from Bill, the only boys Maura had met were at brief meetings at the pool and tennis courts—and Kevin DeAngelo. No! Jill couldn't be thinking of him. The very thought was almost laughable, and Maura immediately pushed it from her mind.

"Well, I wish you luck with Bill," Maura said, "though you certainly have a strange way of going about it. And you don't have to worry about me, you know—he's nice, and friendly, but—"

"I understand perfectly." Jill jumped down from the stall door. "Here's Charlie to sponge down Blackfire. See you later, Barnabas. Tomorrow morning I promise you a ride."

Charlie walked up beside the mare and put down a pail of warm water.

"Thanks, Charlie." Maura smiled. "We worked her pretty hard this morning. If you're busy, though, I can sponge her off."

"No trouble, no trouble at all. What I'm hired for. You young ladies get out and have a good time."

"See you later, Charlie," Jill called over her shoulder. "I've been feeding Barnabas a bunch of carrots, so you might want to lighten up on his feed tonight."

Charlie shook his head. "They spoil them, these girls . . . then wonder why they get fat and lazy."

Chapter 6

The parking lot was nearly full by the time the girls got down to the pool

"I completely forgot to tell you," Maura said, "but Bill said he'd probably be here."

Jill smiled like a cat. "I figured as much."

Whatever she had up her sleeve, Maura thought, her friend certainly wasn't worried about the results.

When they reached poolside, they saw their friends clustered in the usual spot at the far corner.

"Hi, guys," Allison Reilly greeted them. "Come on over—a regular party today."

Bill was there, and Maura glanced over to Jill to see if she'd noticed him, too. He smiled warmly at them both as they dropped their towels and stripped off their beach robes. Jill wore a skimpy, green one-piece, while Maura wore her usual white, shown off to better advantage now that she was acquiring a tan.

"Jill, Maura!" Liz Brooks was bubbling. "I was just telling the other guys... mommy and dad have *finally* agreed to let me have that pool party I've been begging for—right here at the club. Can you come?"

"Don't see why not," Jill chirped. "When is it?"

"July eighteenth. At eight. We'll have food, swimming, dancing on the patio."

"Sounds great! I'll have to check with my aunt, but I'm sure we can come. What do you think, Maura?"

"Fine with me."

Maura found her towel, spread it out, and then grabbed a can of soda someone offered her. Soon Bill came over and sat down between her and Jill, politely dividing his time and his conversation between the two of them. Knowing Jill's feelings, however, Maura did her best to take a back seat.

"You know, Maura," Jill commented a few minutes later, "I was just thinking that we haven't used the diving board yet. Can't let all those hours of swim class go to waste now, can we?"

"I'm not going up alone."

"I'll go with you. How about you, Bill?"

"Okay—though I have a feeling you're trying to shame me."

"Never. You do the best backward somersault I've ever seen!"

Laughing, the three rose and walked down to the deep end of the long pool, where there was both a high and low board. The boards were empty.

"You first, Maura," Jill prodded.

"Why me?"

"Cause this was my idea."

"That's no reason."

"Go on," Jill insisted.

"Okay, okay."

Maura stepped up onto the low board, positioned herself, flexed her toes, took a few running strides, jumped, and executed a perfect jackknife, disappearing under the surface with barely a ripple. She came up at pool's edge, grabbed the ladder, and pointed a finger toward Jill. "Now you!"

"Okay. Jackknives across the board this time—no pun intended." Jill came high off the board, touched her toes, then sent her petite form like an arrow into the water. Bill followed suit.

Maura waited by the board until they were all out and dripping on the concrete. "Well, I'm ready for a doze in the sun."

"Huh-uh," cried Jill. "High-board, first."

"Oh, I don't know. I don't really feel like forward rolls or anything that energetic."

"Then do a simple swan dive. This time gentlemen first. After you watch Bill, maybe you'll get some inspiration."

"I'm game," he shouted from halfway up the ladder. Seconds later he sprang from the board and did a beautiful forward roll and half twist into the water.

"I didn't know he dived so well," Maura remarked as Jill started up the ladder.

Jill's contribution was a simple, clean, forward somersault, executed with grace.

Then it was Maura's turn. Deciding to stick with the swan dive, she stood poised on the board, not realizing what a picture she made with her long, wet hair on her shoulders, her white suit accentuating the tan of her skin. She went off, pushing out in a long arc, bringing her hands slowly forward from her sides to meet over her head, then breaking cleanly into the water. With a few easy strokes, she swam to the side to join her friends.

Grinning as she pulled herself up on the edge, she sked, "Can I go back to my towel now and play lazy?"

"Since there aren't any other boards to try, I guess we'll let you."

"I enjoyed that," Bill said happily as they started walking. "Good idea, Jill."

"Thanks. Want to try it again next time we're all here?"

"Sure—good way to keep in practice."

Rejoining their friends, they stood for a moment, talking, drying off. Bill and Jeff Gates immediately embarked on a conversation about sailing. As Maura listened, she felt Jill's elbow her in the ribs.

"Don't be too obvious, but take a glance over your shoulder to the other side of the pool. I think you'll be interested."

Maura waited a second, then looked to see Kevin DeAngelo staring directly at her.

"He's been there for a while. I think he watched us dive," Jill added in Maura's ear. "Looking good!"

As much as she hated to admit it, Maura had

to agree. Kevin's already olive skin was tanned to a deep tone, making his green eyes that much more sparkling and noticeable. For a second those eyes held Maura's. She was surprised by the strange, exciting thrill that went up her spine. Was she insane to react in this foolish way to someone whose arrogance she couldn't tolerate? He glanced at the group around her, then, turning to the long-haired brunette at his side, he straightened his shoulders and dived into the pool.

"I still say he's a conceited snob," Maura whispered back to Jill, fighting her reaction. "And take a look at that dishy looking brunette."

"Purely decorative. I know her, and she hasn't got a brain in her head."

"Maybe he doesn't want brains."

"I think you're wrong there."

The group began breaking up and going off in their own directions shortly after. Bill said goodbye and left to go sailing. Jill and Maura decided to leave, too. After Kevin's blatant stare, Maura hadn't the courage to turn around to see what he was doing. Obviously he had his hands full with his willowly girlfriend. But as she glanced around the pool, after she'd gathered up her things, she saw that Kevin was gone.

Just as well, she decided. There was no room in her life for someone so arrogant. He was the kind who drew girls as bees were drawn to honey. Maura had no desire to be one of the swarm.

Chapter 7

A few mornings later, the girls were glancing out their bedroom window when a spanking new one-stall horse van pulled into the yard.

"Nice rig," Jill commented.

"Mmm."

"Wonder whose it is? Most of the riders board their horses here."

"Get a load of this," Maura exclaimed getting a glimpse of the van's driver. "If it isn't his 'highness' himself."

"So it is." Jill's eyebrows lifted. "Uncle Alex *did* say he came over to practice. What perfect timing, just when you're ready to go out and have your lesson."

"Oh, be quiet," Maura frowned.

"At least we'll get to see his horse."

Maura snorted disgustedly.

"You really have it in for him. Don't you think you're being a little hasty? You only talked to him once."

"Something about his attitude convinced me it was instant dislike." Maura started to turn from the window. She didn't dare tell Jill about the other strong emotions that stirred inside her whenever he was near.

Kevin jumped down from the driver's seat, then strode purposefully toward the back of the van to unlock and open the half-doors. He was totally unaware of his fascinated audience as he pulled the ramp down into place, secured it, then stepped up inside. A moment later the rump of a chestnut stallion appeared. His rear legs pranced as he was coaxed backward down the ramp. In another second Kevin's dark head reappeared, his hand on the lead rope. Through the open window the girls could hear his soothing tones trying to quiet the stallion, who shook his head nervously and rolled his eyes in mistrust of his new surroundings. "Okay, Challenger, easy now. You've been here before."

Once the stallion was off the ramp and onto solid ground, he seemed to quiet immediately. He lifted his head, and his nostrils flared at the new smells, but he now seemed more curious than fearful.

Alex appeared from around the corner of the house. "Hi, Kevin! You're out early this morning. That's a fine-looking horse, my boy!" His eyes went appreciatively over the horse at the end of the lead.

"He's turned out well. My mother wasn't so sure when he was a two-year-old with that gangling gait, but he's grown into it."

"So it would appear. You've been schooling him at Maple Park?"

"My mother was while I was away at Harvard

—though these last two summers I've been putting him through his paces."

"Planning on riding him in the show?"

"I hope to."

Alex Warren fingered his chin. "Kind of young, don't you think? Only a four-year-old. Not seasoned enough—likely to be skittery."

"It might seem that way now, but once he's facing a course, he puts his mind to it."

"You haven't shown him?"

"No. That's why I'm here to practice," Kevin grinned. "We took him out on a couple of hunts in Virginia last fall. Did well—brought me through and we were in with the kill."

"Then he's used to the confusion of animals around him," Alex Warren said thoughtfully, "but not the human crowd."

"No, but I'm hoping by schooling in your ring, where there's more activity, I can solve that problem."

"Good idea. Feel free—though I can't give you the main ring for the next hour. I'm training my niece's friend, Maura, and Blackfire—both of whom I hope will put a little heat on you in the competitions."

Kevin's eyes showed a glint of interest at the mention of Maura's name, though his expression was carefully controlled to reveal no emotion.

"You can use the smaller ring if you like for about an hour. Then the main ring will be open to all takers."

"Good enough considering you had no idea I was coming."

53

"Well, good ride, my boy." Alex clapped his shoulder. "I've got to see if the horses are ready."

"Ha!" Jill grinned jubilantly, turning from the window to stare at Maura. "Wasn't it worth it? Now you can go down there and show him your stuff. Boy, is he interested!"

"I don't give a darn what he thinks," Maura said unconvincingly.

"You're a liar. Go show him up! And we can watch him, too."

"And he'll know we're watching and probably do no more than put the chestnut through his paces . . . you know, save the good stuff for when we're not around."

"He wouldn't have come over so early if he didn't want us to see. Where else would we be at eight-thirty in the morning?"

Fifteen minutes later Maura was standing in the ring, getting a leg up from Alex into Blackfire's saddle. Jill leaned over the fence, watching.

Maura's stomach was in knots. On the one hand she was excited, wanting to let Kevin see just how good she was; on the other hand, she was quaking, afraid she'd slip up, fail, make a fool of herself. The worst thing was that she felt self-conscious. She could see him in the next ring, already mounted, quieting his stallion, walking him, looking surreptitiously over his shoulder toward her. She couldn't put her best foot forward with him watching. Yet if she wanted that blue ribbon, that was precisely what she would have to do. She felt it strange that the opinions of this arrogant, handsome young man suddenly seemed so important to her.

Alex, naturally, was entirely oblivious to her turmoil. He set her off at a walk, then a posting trot, then a canter, just as though everything was as usual in their morning lesson. At first she couldn't concentrate, but Alex's sharp voice quickly brought her back to the importance of what she was doing. "Heels down! Sit back in that canter! What is this—a circus act?"

She cringed to realize Kevin was hearing his words and probably chuckling.

Okay, Maura, she said to herself, let's get down to business. She forced her mind away from Kevin, to her mare's strides and to her own limbs, and again the magic worked.

She went through the balance of the preliminary warm-up in fine form. Today's lesson was unexpected fences—an unknown course, and the problems that could arise. Alex put her on honor system as she turned her back and he flagged the jumps she was to take. When he told her to turn, she immediately put Blackfire into a canter at the top of the ring, circled to find and face the first red flag that awaited. It was the brush. No problem there. There was plenty of room to see and judge. Thereafter, the run wasn't so easy. Odd fences were marked; a jag across the ring to the double rail; then back to the gate; around the wall and over the barrels; skip the in and out and take the rail; up the center to the white gate. End of course.

Alex was beaming. He sent her out again

on a straight course, over every obstacle. She and Blackfire stayed together and did beautifully. Then Alex had her turn while he altered the course again, marking the first fence with a white flag.

Maura had to reverse and come forward from the opposite direction. Two rails, the wall, a gate, the in and out, skip the brush, over the barrels, turn, come back over the double bar. She stumbled here. She hadn't gauged Blackfire's paces correctly. The mare was a half stride off when she reached the fence. Although Blackfire gallantly pulled herself over, she landed in an off-lead canter, and Maura banged in the saddle. She had to correct the mare, or there would be disaster at the next fence.

Resolutely Maura pulled up the reins. Blackfire could be a quick-change artist but at that moment didn't seem inclined. Maura had to pull her back further, into a trot. Praying that she could change her lead without having to turn Blackfire from the fence, she dug her heel into the mare's left side. Amazing animal that she was, Blackfire double stepped and put out a right lead. Maura sighed in relief. They were still two strides from the next jump, and she could make it. The rider and horse flew over, came up along the outside rail, and met Alex.

His voice was low yet firm. "You corrected that offstride, and I'm proud of you. That's the ingredient it will take to win." He paused for a moment as Maura continued to walk Blackfire in a small circle nearby. "Have you ever thought far enough ahead to consider the National Horse

Show at Madison Square Garden in New York?"

Maura was stupefied. "The National Horse Show? Never!"

"Think of it—though this lesson is not really the place to bring it up."

"But am I good enough?"

"You will be," Alex answered confidently, "with a little practice. And you've got the right horse beneath you."

"It sounds so fantastic—but I don't know."

"We can talk about it later. For now, I want you to run the course again—straight around."

"Yes, sir."

Maura came through magnificently. As she finished her last fence, she wondered what Kevin thought of her runs. Her performance had been good; she could admit that to herself. But was he impressed?

As she led Blackfire from the gate, she looked over to see Kevin studying her. His eyes were narrowed, his expression unreadable. He walked his stallion toward the main ring, entering it only moments after she'd exited.

She began to move away, but Alex motioned and stopped her. "Wait," he said. "Watch the competition."

Maura halted. Kevin had his stallion in a canter. She could see the chestnut's excitement as Kevin turned him toward the first jump. The leashed power of the gleaming muscles was evident as Kevin held the horse firmly in check, releasing the tension on the reins only seconds before the jump, so the mighty animal soared into the air and then landed to again be brought in check for the next fence. Maura sighed as she saw the grace of the stallion. She more than understood the control the rider was exerting over his mount to achieve that effortless picture of fluid motion.

Kevin and Challenger continued around, clearing fences with inches to spare. Every stride was perfect. Kevin was far better than she'd imagined—a real professional. Would she ever look as good?

Yet even as these sentiments flickered through her mind, she determined she was going to beat him. If it took all the practice in the world, she would!

Chapter 8

From then on Maura saw Kevin frequently at Warren Farm—sometimes in the early mornings, but more often than not in the afternoon. He'd lead his already tacked stallion out, then practice for an hour in the ring.

No one knew the courses that would eventually be set up for the show, but many local people wanted to practice in order to familiarize themselves with the ring. Of the future participants, Kevin was the only one who caught

Maura's interest. Yet she was still irked by his arrogance and made no attempt to initiate a conversation.

She had no way of knowing, of course, but her behavior intrigued Kevin. With his looks he was used to girls going out of their way to capture his attention. But this girl was different. The little he'd seen of her, he'd liked—her graceful beauty, the sparkle of intelligence in her eyes, the warmth of the wide smile, which never seemed to be for him. He found himself being drawn to her. He watched for her when he arrived at the farm. Sometimes he would see her walking around the side of the barn, across the lawn, and through the kitchen door. In vain he'd wait for her to reappear; only when he gave up could he direct his attention to his practice session. Other times, as he passed the open stable doors, he would spy her in the center aisle vigorously grooming her mare. She didn't look up and seemed completely oblivious to everything except her horse. The few times they did meet face to face, the barely perceptible nod of recognition she sent his way inflamed his curiosity further. How was he to get through to her?

Then one day, as he led Challenger into the ring, he saw Maura among several other riders gathered there, training on her own. She was on the opposite side of the ring, her back toward him, so his entrance went unnoticed.

Mounting quickly, he maneuvered Challenger so they were only a few paces behind Maura and her mare, though still unobserved. Gradually he closed the distance between them until he came up on her left flank. It would be impossible for her to escape him now without outright rudeness. As she glanced down to the mare's right front shoulder to check her diagonal, he spoke.

"Hello, Maura."

At the deep voice sounding unexpectedly in her ear, Maura jerked around and faced him as he drew alongside.

"At last we ride together," he said quietly. "I've watched you practice a couple of times. You're good."

Disconcerted, Maura dropped her eyes. His tone was friendly—a fact that was enough to leave Maura bewildered. "Thank you," she said sincerely.

"You're welcome."

"Quite a compliment coming from as excellent a rider as you."

"But well deserved." The smile he gave her was open and honest.

In her nervousness Maura gripped the reins more tightly. Blackfire wagged her head in protest. "You're here to practice?"

"I've been around most every day for almost two weeks."

"Oh, really?" Did he notice the flush in her cheeks brought by this lie, Maura wondered?

"You're usually busy," he said mildly.

"Jill and I go down to the club a lot."

"I saw you there one day, too."

"Did you? Oh, I remember. You were with a dark-haired girl, weren't you?"

"An old friend."

Maura found she couldn't look too long at his profile without feeling flustered. She focused her eyes instead over Blackfire's head, at the dirt track.

"I saw you and your friends dive," he continued. "That was a good one you made off the high board."

"The swan dive? Thanks."

"Bill Peters was with you, wasn't he?"

"Uh-huh. You know him?"

"Vaguely. He's a good friend of yours, I gather. You dating him?"

"Bill? No—I mean, he's a nice guy...."

Kevin was silent for a moment. "Just wondering. I've seen him here a few times, too."

"He drops by to say hello—he lives nearby." Why was she explaining herself to him? It was none of his business.

But Kevin was already changing the subject. "How have you enjoyed your summer so far?"

"What more could I ask? Living at the back door of a stable, training for a show."

"I imagine we'll be competing against each other."

"So Mr. Warren told me."

"I intend to give you a run for your money."

"So do I."

He laughed. "At least I'll know all these hours of practicing are worth it."

"You can't really be worried."

"Why not?"

"You don't strike me as the type. Besides,

you've had a lot more experience—my background has been purely amateur. And with that beautiful horse..."

He glanced down at Blackfire's gleaming sides. "What about yours?"

"Yes, she's a beauty," Maura agreed. "But she's not mine, and I'll only have these few more weeks to practice."

"Alex Warren seems to think you've got what it takes. But in any case you'll have fun trying."

"You saying I'm not going to make it?"

"Of course not. But if you don't..."

"I only think positively."

He laughed, and the sound broke through the afternoon air, causing another rider to turn and look at them. Neither Kevin nor Maura noticed, however.

"I really should give Blackfire a break," Maura said suddenly. "She's been worked too long today."

"What we're doing now can't be considered working."

"No, but she had a rough lesson this morning."

"A shame when Challenger's only started to limber up. You riding tomorrow?"

"Definitely, for my lesson."

"Then maybe we'll see each other." The tone of his voice told her that it was his intention they would.

As they neared the gate, Maura turned off.

"Good talking to you," he called.

Glancing back over her shoulder, she gave

him an unexpected smile. "Same here." Then she dismounted, unhooked the gate, and walked through.

She didn't know what to make of it. Kevin singling her out... going out of his way to talk to her. Of course, she wasn't going to let it go to her head. Or was she...

They met again the next day in the training ring. Kevin came up just as Maura was finishing up a session with Blackfire.

"Mind if I walk with you?" he asked as she led Blackfire from the ring.

"No," she answered after a pause, "c'mon along."

Silently they walked Blackfire toward the stable. Maura couldn't imagine what Kevin wanted. She felt him staring at her. Unlike the day they had met, however, his gaze seemed friendly and open.

"Tell me about yourself, Maura," he asked finally. "Where are you from?"

"Easton. About forty miles south of here."

"You have your own stables?"

"No."

"But you ride so well."

"I've been riding for as long as I can remember. It's just that my parents travel quite a bit, and it wouldn't be convenient to keep a horse at home. Then again, I'm away at school so much of the time."

"Oh? Where do you go?" Kevin reached up and plucked a leaf from one of the low-hanging tree branches.

"Maryvale—a small private girls' school just outside Easton."

"Don't they have stables?" He seemed surprised.

"No. My father's offered to buy me a hunter to be boarded at the club where I take lessons, but how often could I ride? I didn't think it would be fair to the animal, so I train on the club's hacks twice a week. They're not all that bad, and actually it's good experience to get the feel of a different mount every few weeks."

"How do you know the Warrens?"

Conscious of his observing glance, Maura looked away and directed her eyes toward the woodland in the distance. She was still wary of him and didn't entirely trust his assured manner. She refused to believe he was sincerely interested.

"Through Jill. We go to school together, and she's up here every summer. Until this year, I spent every summer traveling with my parents."

"Like me," he said thoughtfully, "except I could spend certain summers here even when my parents were away. Two servants who came over with my father from Italy are around to keep an eye on me."

"Your father's Italian? I should have guessed from your last name."

"Yes. He's been here twenty-some-odd years. His family owns an export business based in Florence—paintings, artworks, things like that. He was sent to New York to run the American branch."

"How did you come to Southbury? It's not an easy commute to New York." Maura was surprised how easy it was to talk to Kevin.

"My mother's idea. She grew up spending her time between Connecticut and my uncle's breeding farm in Ireland." He chuckled. "I've heard the story many times. My mother met my father through a mutual friend while she was traveling in Italy. After they married, they lived for a while in Florence, but when my father found out he was being sent to the States, she begged him to find her a place in the country where she could keep her horses. She knew Connecticut—this area—and Maple Park was on the market."

"Sounds romantic."

He shrugged. "I suppose it is. My mother rides every day when she's home. My father's in New York most of the time running the business, but they have an apartment there, and she goes down often. Dad comes up here on weekends."

"So that's where you get your horsemanship."

He nodded. "From what my father tells me, she had me on the back of a pony before I could walk. That may be exaggeration—he's not a horseman and would rather see me put my mind toward the export business."

"Is that what you are going to do?" Maura asked.

"I'm not sure. I don't want to disappoint him, but horses are in my blood, and antiques aren't. It's far easier for me to judge the qualities of a good hunter than the beauties of a Tuscany vase or a piece of Venetian glass."

"The Italian in you comes out in other ways," Maura teased.

"What do you mean?" His brows lifted.

"Italian men are noted for their 'macho' instincts."

"Is that an insult or compliment?"

"Take it as you wish."

"From you—an insult."

Maura laughed in spite of herself. "Actually I was thinking that you're too aware of your attributes."

"So I'm egotistical?"

"Sometimes—"

"Don't you think you come across that way, too?" he burst in before she could finish.

"What do you mean?"

"You're aloof—as though you can't stand people—me in particular."

"No, that's not it. I'm shy, I just don't know how to express myself sometimes."

"You really expect me to believe that?"

"Why not?"

"Because you're pretty. You must have had enough guys tell you so that you know it."

"No, I haven't. As a matter of fact, there haven't been any boys around at all."

"I still don't believe it."

"Suit yourself." Maura said. "Let's change the subject. So where do you go to school?"

"Harvard. I'll be starting my second year in the fall."

"And then into the family business?"

66

"Maybe. But what I'd really like to do is breed racehorses."

"That takes a lot of capital."

"I have it," he said more arrogantly than he meant.

"You mean, your *father* has it," Maura corrected him.

"So you think I'm a spoiled brat?"

"If I go into music, I'll be doing it on my own, except for college tuition."

"And your father won't be helping at all?" Kevin sneered.

"I've already determined when I'm old enough I'm going to stand on my own two feet."

"My, such independence."

"Better than being tied to the apron strings!"

"Do you realize we're arguing?"

His words sobered Maura. She hardly knew Kevin, and they'd been discussing such personal things. She flushed. "We are, aren't we?"

"Why?"

"I don't know."

"I've been trying to cultivate warm feelings." He grinned sheepishly, "and here I am blowing my whole scene."

There was no answer Maura was ready to give to that statement. She continued to hold Blackfire's reins and walk to the stable door.

Kevin's voice was soft. "Sorry. And I don't usually say that."

"I didn't think you did."

"Why are you so different?"

"Am I?" Though Maura's heart wasn't beating with its normal regularity, she wasn't about to give away any more of her feelings than she already had.

Kevin suddenly stopped at the stable's entrance. Since Maura was walking directly at his side, she stopped, too, and gave him a mystified look.

"Let's not argue anymore, Maura. I'll see you soon." His brilliant green eyes stared into hers for an instant, and then he was gone.

As she walked Blackfire to his stall, she wondered about their conversation, about the effect of his words, the effect he was having upon her. Her emotions were a crazy jumble of happiness and anger. Parts of their conversation had made her furious, yet when she had looked into his eyes, she had seen a boy she could possibly like—maybe even very much.

Chapter 9

Maura was determined to put Kevin from her mind, but the next afternoon as Jill and she were turning into the club driveway, they met him as he was driving out in his gray Porsche. Unexpectedly he stopped his car beside theirs, waving his hand. Jill, thinking quickly, hit the brakes.

"Tennis or swimming today?" He leaned one arm through his open window.

Jill answered spontaneously. "Too warm for tennis."

Maura felt her stomach flipping for no reason at all.

"Tell me about it," he returned. "I just finished two sets."

"Why don't you join us for a swim?"

"Love to, but my mother wants me to run some errands. And I'm already late." His eyes seemed to go to Maura, though Jill was between them. "I'll have to squeeze in a few laps later at home. Hi, Maura."

"Hi, Kevin."

"Tomorrow morning?"

"I'll be riding."

He revved his engine and shifted into first. "Then I'll catch you later." He smiled, and the gray Porsche whizzed away.

When he was gone, Jill grabbed her friend's wrist. "What did I tell you? He's crazy about you!"

Could Maura dare to believe his interest was sincere?

Kevin was at the farm the following morning. Maura saw his van pull in midway through her lesson while she was taking a breather. He didn't make an appearance at the ring, however, until her lesson was over and she was leading Blackfire out. Trotting Challenger across the gravel, he stopped beside her.

"Good morning."

"Beautiful one, isn't it?" she answered breezily.

"I only have a minute," he said, smiling softly. "I want to get in some practice while the ring is empty, but in case we don't get to talk later, I wanted to ask if you'd like to go riding with me tomorrow afternoon. Not in the ring, but cross-country, out in the woods. We can start out from here. What do you say?"

Maura stared at him a moment, shocked that he was actually asking her for a date. Did she really want to go? Wasn't this contrary to everything she'd promised herself about not being one of the many bees buzzing around this handsome young man? Yet wasn't her earlier image of Kevin as an arrogant egoist a bit unfair as well? Wasn't he showing her another side—a warm and friendly side? Or was that only a pose he'd assumed because he found her a challenge he'd thus far been unable to conquer?

Finally, she nodded, "Yes . . . all right . . . I will."

"Good." His expression was one of delight. "One o'clock okay? I'll bring Challenger over in the van."

"Fine."

"See you then." His brilliant green eyes caught hers, and held them, until in confusion Maura smiled quickly and hurried away.

That evening when she told Jill about Kevin's invitation, Jill immediately began to dance excitedly about the room, grabbing Maura's hands. "Didn't I tell you? Fantastic! Fantastic! The most sought-after guy in Southbury, and he's going out with my best friend!"

"Jill, it's only for a ride," Maura protested.

"But it won't end there. This is only the beginning."

Beginning of what? Maura wondered silently. Did she really want to think ahead? She felt much safer just taking each day as it came, especially since she wasn't sure just what she felt for Kevin. Yes, it was oddly exciting to be with him; her senses felt alive and electric. It was impossible not to be flattered by his attentiveness. She had to admit that she *wanted* to be with him, yet she was afraid to look too deeply into herself and her emotions.

Bill Peters came over to the farm the next morning as the girls were out on the back lawn having a lemonade.

"Well, you two look lazy."

"We are," Jill laughed. "Too nice a day to think of doing anything constructive."

"I'm glad to hear that because I was just going to ask you both if you'd like to take a ride down to Candlewood with me. A good friend of mine has a nice-sized sailboat moored at the lake and invited me and anyone I want to bring for the day."

Jill's face immediately lit with interest. "I'm game."

"Maura?"

"Gee, Bill, it sounds like fun, but I've already made plans."

"Oh." His face fell momentarily.

"Don't look so disappointed," Jill piped up. "We both know you're upset because you'll only have one ravishing beauty on your arm instead of two—but, heck, you can't have everything." She preened, fluffing her reddish-blond hair, and Bill couldn't help laughing.

"Maybe some other time," Maura added as Jill ran inside to tell her aunt her plans, and to get ready. She returned a few minutes later with a windbreaker over her arm.

"Well, I'm ready," she said exuberantly. "We might as well take my car since it's right here."

"Are you trying to tell me?" he intoned, "that you don't care for my elegant roadster?"

"Of course not." Her eyes widened, then she winked, "Though I don't know about the elegant part."

"Okay, I know when I'm beat. Just throw me your keys. I'll drive."

Maura waved them off as they climbed into the red sports car. She was delighted to see them chattering happily as they pulled out of the drive.

Promptly at one, Maura, looking pretty in a lightweight rose shirt and jeans, came into the back yard and took a seat in one of the lawn chairs. She'd only been waiting a moment when Kevin's van pulled in. She rose to meet him, then feeling self-conscious and awkward, went to lean against the trunk of one of the maples as he parked and led Challenger from the van.

"Hello there." He smiled when he spotted her. "You look nice."

"Thank you."

"A perfect afternoon for riding—cool and clear. Is Blackfire ready?"

"I'll be taking Snappers. He's tacked and waiting in the barn. Blackfire had a real workout this morning."

"We'll collect him on our way to the field then. Alex doesn't mind us riding up into the woods?"

"No, he thought it was a great idea—said I needed to get out and play a little." She laughed, trying to force herself to relax. She could feel her hands trembling and clenched them together behind her back, so Kevin wouldn't notice. Her stomach was filled with butterflies. This was completely ridiculous, she scolded herself. She'd ridden with Kevin before. But this was different—entirely different.

Once they'd both mounted, they headed out across the green pastureland. It wasn't long before they were up into the hills and on the winding trails.

The trees were in full, leafy bloom; the woods smelled damp and sweet from mulched leaves and moss. A stream was gurgling over a rocky bed within earshot but out of sight. Birds were in the trees calling to each other, their trills sweet and clear. Everything was as it should have been for a mid-July afternoon.

Neither one said a word as they concentrated on maneuvering their mounts up the narrow path, avoiding rocks, ducking branches. Yet Maura began to relax a little, as what she had sensed before became a certain fact in her mind—there was a lot more to Kevin DeAngelo than she'd seen on the surface. True, he was a bit conceited, but that was no more than could be expected in someone who'd been showered with attention all his life. She was beginning to understand that underneath, there was a real person with doubts and insecurities, as well as a person who could be warm and considerate. She found herself unbending and felt an attraction to Kevin she didn't want to admit to herself.

They'd ridden for quite a while. With Kevin leading, Maura had paid little attention to their direction until she found herself staring down into the meadow on the DeAngelo property where Jill and she had first met him. Kevin continued on down to the willow-draped pond. Then he suggested they dismount and walk the horses for a while.

"This is such a lovely place," Maura commented quietly.

"I've always liked it. I come here when I want to be alone, to think, to make a decision."

"I guess you miss it when you go off to college."

"No more than usual. I boarded at Hotchkiss and was only home on vacations. It's no different at Harvard."

"You must have had good grades."

"I've managed to get by."

Maura was silent, feeling strangely peaceful.

"Is there really no one in particular you date at home?" Kevin asked suddenly.

"No, I don't date at all."

He shook his head. "That's so hard to believe."

"Why?"

"Because you're pretty, and you're pleasant to be with. I have this picture in my mind of guys falling all over you."

"You have a vivid imagination." Maura laughed.

"But what if the right guy came along?"

"I suppose I'd be interested." She shrugged. "I don't really think about it."

"I've never met anyone like you." He studied Maura's profile as she stared ahead, oblivious to his gaze. "Most girls your age are boy-crazy, but you're so self-contained."

She looked up at him, puzzled. "What do you mean by self-contained?"

"Complete within yourself," he explained. "As opposed to your friend, Jill, who seems to need people around her all the time. You don't."

"I like to be alone—sometimes." Maura's eyes returned to the landscape, the tufts of grass under her feet. "A lot of the things I enjoy I can do by myself—riding, piano playing, reading. And, as I told you before, I'm shy at times. I can't talk to people I don't know very easily. But you're different than I am, I think."

"My turn to ask why."

"You know how to be charming—you know what to say. Even if you're not interested, people think you are. You can talk and pretend, while I close up into a little shell." Maura paused, then decided to be honest. "That's part of the reason I don't entirely trust you."

75

Kevin stopped in his tracks. "I think you'd better explain."

Maura loosened her hold on her horse's reins as he dropped his head to crop the grass. "I don't mean to insult you—it's just that I haven't been around all that much."

He was very serious as he gazed at her. "You don't have anything to fear from me, Maura. I promise you that."

"I'm very naive." She laughed, self-consciously.

"That's part of your charm. You don't put on airs. The real you is always there for the world to see."

"I've never analyzed myself so thoroughly."

He looked at her for a moment, then asked, "How do you feel about me, Maura?"

She was surprised at the question, but she answered honestly. "I like you."

"I was afraid you still considered me the ultimate snob."

"I did at first."

"I know. But now?"

"I'm changing my mind."

He took her free hand, gently squeezed her fingers, released them, and lifted his hand to touch her cheek.

She was startled by the warm thrill she felt at his touch. This couldn't be happening. Finding herself and Kevin DeAngelo in such a situation had never been part of her imaginings. Yet he was looking at her with a definite warmth in his green eyes. She looked away, confused. Gently, he lifted her chin, bent down and kissed her softly. Then he put his arms around her and drew her close to him.

Maura heard his low sigh and felt a headiness as his fingers tangled in her shining, soft hair. A strange confusion whirled in her brain ... the old, cool logic warring with a new sensation, that of physical yearning.

Kevin felt her tense in his arms, and released her. Gazing into her eyes, he asked, "What's wrong?"

"I don't know exactly."

"I think I do." His tone was understanding and kind. "We'll walk a little longer, then we'll go back. Do you mind if I hold your hand?" He smiled softly.

"No." A surge of relief flooded through her.

He was silent as they continued their short journey around the pond, yet words didn't need to be spoken, for at that moment there was a bond of understanding between them.

"Maura," he said at last as he gave her a leg into her saddle, "I meant what I said. I really like you."

She paused. "I like you, too."

"Do you mean that?"

"I do."

"I'll see you tomorrow?"

She nodded.

He seemed satisfied, leapt onto Challenger's back, and they cantered off toward the Warren farm.

Chapter 10

With the barriers down between them, Kevin and Maura's relationship rapidly strengthened into close friendship. Maura found herself thinking of him increasingly—in fact, the only time his face didn't penetrate into her thoughts was during her hour's lesson each morning when all was blocked from her mind but her performance.

Though she and Kevin talked frequently of the show, they didn't discuss that they would be competing for the same ribbon. Although Kevin encouraged her and praised her, in the back of her mind Maura realized that he didn't really take her seriously. She was convinced he was so supremely confident of his own riding ability that he never considered her a threat, and Maura didn't press the issue. She was too involved with the new emotions she was feeling. Over and over, she thought of his kiss and the warmth of his arms about her. She relished the heady sensations she had each time she saw him, and she wanted them to continue. Yet she was uneasy, too, afraid of her feelings and where they might lead.

Jill approached her on the subject one night as they were lying in their room listening to records.

"You saw Kevin this morning?"

"Yes, your uncle gave us a joint lesson. Do you believe it?"

"Once, yes. It was an experiment since he knows you'll be up against each other in the show, but he won't do it again." Jill paused, toying with one of her curls. "You and Kevin were talking afterward. Comparing notes?"

"Not really. We don't talk much about riding against each other. It's a touchy subject."

"I can imagine. Not to be nosy, but what *were* you talking about?"

"Just general things..."

Jill grinned impishly. "I see my plans are working out well. Everything's going according to schedule."

"Then was Kevin the mystery boy you had in mind for me all along?"

Jill nodded. "Only it's going better than even I expected. He's nuts for you."

"I guess he does like me," Maura admitted.

"Ha! It's more than 'like' with this guy," Jill exclaimed. "Geez, he can't take his eyes off you when you're in the ring."

"You're exaggerating."

"Remember I'm watching, while your attention is on Blackfire and Uncle Alex. How do you feel about him?"

"I like him."

"That's all?"

"Oh, Jill." Maura sighed. "I don't know what to think."

"Maybe you're in love!"

Frowning, Maura flipped over on her stomach. "This isn't love."

"You like to be with him, right?"

"Well, yes."

"You think about him all the time? Get excited when you know he's coming over?"

"Look, Jill, it can't be love. I'm not ready for it. I don't even know what it is. And I have too many things I want to do."

"And who doesn't? Didn't your mother ever tell you anything?"

"Now, stop it, Jill. I know the facts of life. All I'm telling you is that I've always had other things on my mind besides boys. I didn't plan on this, and I don't know if I'm ready."

"And who does? Take Bill and me. I never dreamed when we were playing in the mud together as kids that I'd feel the way I do now about him. For the moment my feelings may be one-sided, but that won't last forever. He's going to appreciate me someday."

"He already does."

"You noticed, too?"

Maura nodded.

"Well, that wasn't the point I was trying to make. What I'm trying to say is that there's a future, and we're both growing up—and there's nothing wrong with liking a guy. Someday you might even marry one."

"A long time in the future."

"What's wrong with dating one now?"

Maura shrugged. "Nothing, I guess. It's just—it's just that there are other things I want to do."

"So what? Where is it written that Maura Langdon can't have a boyfriend? And ride and play the piano and do anything else she wants to do?"

Maura looked down at the white bedspread, as confused as ever about her feelings for Kevin.

"Listen, you jerk," Jill said in a lighter tone, "every girl in Southbury would kill to be in your shoes. I'm only telling you to try to appreciate that fact. Understand?"

Chapter 11

The evening of Liz Brooks's pool party was warm and balmy. As the girls dressed to be at the club by eight, dusk gave way to the silver darkness of a moon rising in a star-spangled sky.

As much as she tried to deny it, Maura was alive with excitement. This was the first time she and Kevin would be seeing each other in the evening, amid a large group of people. He'd asked her to meet him there, but there would be so many other girls there, too. Would he give

Maura all his attention, or would he save some of it for other girls—that brunette?

Maura spent a lot of time getting ready, brushing her hair until it glistened, lightly applying mascara to her long lashes, a bit of blusher to her tanned cheeks, lipstick to her lips, perfume behind her ears and on her wrists. She wore a new black and white cutaway swimsuit under a long white halter beach gown.

"Wow," Jill teased. "You're going to knock his eyes out tonight."

"You look pretty good yourself," Maura answered, her eyes appreciatively widening at her friend's designer two-piece suit.

Jill gave another brush to her strawberry curls, then wrapped herself in a long, multicolored sarong. She fastened it, took a last look in the mirror, then asked, "Ready?" Maura nodded.

The Warrens were waiting in the living room as the girls came down the stairs.

"My, my," Alex said, "had I realized two such gorgeous ladies were living under my roof, I would have had the watchdogs out before now."

"You both look lovely," Lorna Warren agreed. "Have a wonderful time."

"I don't want you out too late," Alex Warren warned. "I don't mean to sound like a scolding father but—"

"Of course, you don't." Jill skipped over to kiss his cheek. "But you'll worry. We'll be home by twelve at the latest. Promise."

"Have a great time."

"We will."

At the club parking lot, Maura searched for Kevin's Porsche, but in the deepening darkness she couldn't find it.

"Don't worry," Jill assured her as if reading her mind. "He'll be here. I see Bill's old jalopy over by the fence. I don't know why he feels such a sentimental attachment to that pile of tin."

"Maybe because he fixed it up himself," Maura said of the 1930s gray-primed roadster that had been a rotting heap behind his father's barn before Bill had set his mind to repairing it. "When he's finished, it'll be a classic."

"Guess I don't appreciate the finer things in life. But what's one small fault when I'm perfect in every other way?" Jill said striking an exaggerated pose.

"You're a nut." Maura laughed.

Lanterns had been strung from the tree branches in the grassy area surrounding the pool, giving the grounds a fairy-tale quality. Speakers sent rock music wafting continuously into the night air. Already the poolside was crowded, and Maura and Jill wove their way on the outskirts.

Liz Brooks ran over. "Hi, guys. Welcome. Some crowd, huh? There's soda and eats over on the table." She pointed under the trees. "And I think I saw Bill...oh, yes, over at the other side of the pool. Hank and Craig Reeves are having a race. Well, have fun."

"Thanks, Liz. See you later."

Before they got much closer to the pool, they noticed that the crowd was moving away from the water's edge, surrounding the victorious Craig Reeves. A few of his friends slapped him on the back. "What's next?" someone called out. "How about a little diving?" Several young men took up the suggestion.

On the patio behind the clubhouse a few couples had begun dancing; still others had congregated around the refreshment table. As Maura looked around the crowd, trying to spot Kevin, Bill Peters came up at her elbow. He had tried several times in the past two weeks to talk to Maura alone, but without being too obvious, Maura had managed to avoid an encounter. She knew he was interested in her, but she didn't know how to tell him she wasn't, without being rude and hurting his feelings.

There was no avoiding Bill now, though, as he smiled warmly. "You're looking nice tonight."

"Thank you."

"Where's Jill? You came alone?"

"She's here someplace—though I couldn't tell you precisely *where*. We were separated."

"Not surprising in this zoo. Say, where've you been the last few days?

"Riding, mostly."

"I guess the training must be rough."

"I want to be my best."

As part of Maura's mind concentrated on Bill's conversation, the rest of it wondered whether Kevin had arrived. Her eyes automatically searched the faces in the crowd for a sight of him.

"Actually," Bill was saying quietly. "I'm glad we're alone for a minute."

His tone caught Maura's attention, and she looked up at him.

He appeared a little flustered, and gave her a lopsided grin. "I've been wanting to ask you this for a while. What I was wondering... this Saturday night, if you're not busy, would you like to go to the movies with me? There's a couple of good shows playing in Danbury."

Though Maura had almost expected the question, she was tongue-tied. All she could think about was Jill's pain should she learn that Bill had asked her for a date. She stumbled. "Well, it's very nice of you to ask, Bill..." She never had a chance to finish her sentence.

Kevin DeAngelo strode up at that moment, stopping at Maura's side. His voice broke through the air. "Hate to have to disappoint you, Peters, but Maura already has a date with me this Saturday."

Bill was startled. Maura swung around, her mouth dropping.

"Sorry to walk up on you like that," Kevin continued smoothly, "but I've been looking all over for you, Maura." He laid a possessive hand on her arm. "I thought you were supposed to meet me."

As the connection began clicking in his mind, Bill looked back and forth between the two of them. "Oh... I see." His voice was suddenly cool. "I didn't realize."

"Bill—" Maura began.

"Excuse me, but I think I'll go find Jill."

Without another word, he backed off and walked hurriedly away.

Maura turned on Kevin. "What's the big idea? You had no right to do that! And who says we're going out on Saturday!"

"Were you going to date Peters?" Kevin's eyes flashed.

"No, but you might have had the decency to let me tell him that myself!"

"Maura, listen, we can't talk here. Walk with me for a minute.'

"I'm anxious to hear your excuse," Maura said angrily as he led her away under the trees, out of the lantern light. "I imagine it's a good one."

"It is! I was jealous."

"Jealous? Of what?"

"You agreed to meet me here. When I arrived, not only weren't you around, but when I found you, you were on the verge of accepting a date with another guy."

"I already told you I wasn't!"

"How was I to know that? Don't you think I had reason to be angry?"

"Absolutely not! You have no right to interfere in my life."

"We've had some good times together recently. I thought there was an understanding between us. I thought you were beginning to care about me."

"Well, I am. I like you, Kevin, but that doesn't mean you can direct my life according to your plans."

"Maura, listen, I'm sorry. I have a hot temper at times, and I react without thinking."

"Obviously."

"But there's a reason."

"I can't begin to see one," Maura asserted stubbornly.

"When I first met you, you really attracted me," Kevin's tone became softer. "You were so pretty, a fantastic rider, but so cool and collected. Initially I guess I only wanted to see what was underneath that cool exterior. I didn't think you'd ever relent and warm up to me, but finally you did. And I liked what I saw. And I like it more and more as each day goes by."

Maura stared at him. They were far away from the pool now; only the moonlight slanting through the tree branches lit their way over the lawn.

"That's why I lost my head. The way I feel about you, I just couldn't stand to see you with someone else."

"Oh." The word was barely more than a sigh as it escaped Maura's lips.

His hands gently took her shoulders as he stopped and stared down at her averted face. "Maura?" He took her chin and made her look at him. "Does what I'm saying upset you?"

"Yes."

"You must have guessed how I feel. I've tried to go slowly—you didn't seem ready for anything but friendship."

"I wasn't."

"And now?"

"I don't know." She turned away from his stare. "I need time to think."

"I'll give you time."

Maura's thoughts were racing, yet the touch of his hands, the sound of his soft voice sent a warm tingle coursing up and down her spine. She couldn't deny his words thrilled her. But was she ready to go beyond friendship?

"Maura," he pleaded. "I'm really sorry about earlier."

"I'm not angry anymore, Kevin," Maura said quietly.

He gazed down at her in the moonlight. "I want to see as much of you as I can," he whispered. "And that date for Saturday... you interested?"

Maura nodded.

"Great," Kevin beamed. "Have you ever seen a polo match?"

"No, I haven't."

"Really? With your horsey background?"

"I'm the horsey one, remember, not my parents. They've never followed the polo circuit."

"Well, you're going to see one on Saturday. Then we'll catch a bite afterward."

"Sounds terrific," Maura answered.

There was only the whisper of the breeze in the trees as their gazes locked. Then Kevin shook his head quickly as though bringing himself back to his surroundings. "We'd better get back to the party. Want to dance?"

"Sure."

They were both smiling as they moved to ward the lantern light.

Chapter 12

Their date that Saturday was beyond anything Maura had anticipated. Kevin stopped for a few minutes to talk to the Warrens before helping Maura into his waiting car. They were pleased he was taking Maura out as they'd known him and his family for years.

Maura and Kevin cheered themselves hoarse urging the local polo team to victory. Later they had dinner at one of the old country inns in the area.

"My parents and I come here often," Kevin said. "The food's excellent."

With polished charm he ordered for them, Maura leaving the decision in his hands. She wasn't disappointed; the meal was perfect, and Kevin's leisurely conversation left her perfectly at ease. She began to think that maybe Jill was right, maybe she was falling in love with him.

After dinner, they strolled around the inn's beautifully landscaped grounds.

"They have an old-fashioned footbridge in the back over the river," Kevin suggested. "For people like us."

He took her hand and led her down the path under the softly glowing lamplight.

"You come here often?" Maura asked, strongly aware of his touch but trying to be casual.

Kevin grinned. "Not for walks in the moonlight, with a beautiful girl at my side."

They walked halfway across the bridge and stopped, leaning on the sturdy wooden rail to gaze down at the rippling water beneath.

"What are you thinking, Maura?"

"I'm not really thinking about anything—just feeling good."

"You had a nice time today?"

"Yes, wonderful!"

"So did I. Want to go riding with me tomorrow? We can have a picnic."

"All right. I'd like that."

"And the next day?"

"The next."

Throughout the following two weeks, Maura walked as if she were treading on satin-lined clouds. Everything was perfect, exactly as it would be if she were living out a daydream. Every morning and every afternoon she and Kevin were together, riding, swimming, playing tennis. Without conciously considering her reactions, she delighted in his laughter and his playfulness. She also began to appreciate his more serious moods of silent thoughtfulness and the intelligence hidden behind his handsome face. Maura had to pinch herself at times to make sure it wasn't all a dream.

The only doubts to burst Maura's bubble were Lorna Warren's kindly but cautioning words.

"I realize he's a handsome boy—almost too

handsome—but in a few weeks you'll both be going back to school. You still have a lot to do before getting serious with a boy."

"Yes, I know, Mrs. Warren. But Kevin and I are just close friends. I haven't thought of anything serious."

"But what's on *his* mind?"

"I'm not sure. We haven't really talked about it," Maura admitted.

"Kevin's a nice boy. Both Alex and I like him very much, but he's older than you, Maura, and has had far more experience. Summer romances can sometimes be painful, and none of us want to see you hurt."

"I understand, and thank you for talking to me."

Maura, shying away from self-examination, quickly assured herself that her relationship with Kevin wasn't all *that* serious. Still, a nagging worry played at her mind. Kevin was always thoughtful and considerate, charming, so interesting to talk to, and they had so much in common. But lately he seemed to be pushing her to make more of a commitment to him—and she knew she wasn't ready.

At least when it came to the upcoming horse show, Maura's feet were planted firmly on the ground. Afraid Kevin's presence would interfere with her concentration, she'd asked him not to come around until after her morning's lesson, and he'd good-naturedly agreed.

Alex Warren's eyes twinkled mischievously when he spied Kevin's van pulling into the drive promptly at ten-fifteen each day. He said nothing to Maura except to comment slyly one morning. "What I'm wondering about are the fireworks that might erupt when you face each other in the show ring. I don't think he realizes how good you are."

"I don't think he does either—or at least he won't let himself believe it," Maura admitted.

"He's in for a rude shock, Maura. He's a proud young man who won't take kindly to being beaten."

"I may not beat him."

"There's a good chance you may." Then suddenly he frowned and peered at Maura. "You're not, I hope, considering letting him win."

"Of course not!" Maura was genuinely amazed. "I'd never do that!"

"Good. And don't let it sneak into your mind. You've got too much talent to waste it that foolishly."

One afternoon Maura and Kevin were in the barn, grooming their horses after riding.

"I'd like you to come over to the house with me tomorrow afternoon," Kevin said unexpectedly. "Dad's up from New York for a few days, and he and Mother would like to meet you."

"How do they know about me?"

"I may have mentioned a word or two, here and there," he said teasingly.

"I'll be a nervous wreck."

"Why? My parents aren't ogres, you know. They're a couple of pretty nice, down-to-earth people."

"I'm sure they are, but how would you feel if you were meeting my parents for the first time?"

He brought his brush in a long sweep over Challenger's rump. "I don't know. I've always been fairly comfortable with adults."

"Well, I haven't. I've always been afraid I'll say something outrageous and have my mother give me one of her glaring 'wait until you get home' looks."

"Somehow, I can't picture you doing or saying anything outrageous—you're too reserved and well mannered. What do you say? Come for lunch, then spend the afternoon."

"Of course, I'll come."

He stepped over to give her a quick peck on the cheek. "I'll pick you up at eleven-thirty."

After Maura had cooled out Blackfire and put her in her stall the next morning, she went up to shower and change into a cotton skirt and full-sleeved silk blouse, glad after all that she'd brought along something other than jeans and riding clothes.

Jill sat on her bed munching an apple as Maura dressed, applied her makeup, and combed her hair.

"Meeting his parents...big time!" Jill whistled.

"Jill, please, I'm nervous enough already."

"Then let me tell you something to take your mind off yourself. Bill asked me to go to the movies on Wednesday night."

Maura swirled around. "Really? Oh, Jill, that's wonderful. I thought he'd been paying more attention to you lately."

Maura was genuinely happy for her friend. She only prayed that Jill never learned Bill had asked her out first; prayed that his invitation to Jill wasn't a matter of settling for second best. She thought that surely Bill must realize how much he had in common with Jill. How could he help but be caught up by her lively good nature, warm heart and pixielike beauty?

"Yes." Jill winked. "You see, things are going precisely according to plan."

"You sure you don't have a crystal ball hidden somewhere?"

"Nothing so exciting. Only a touch of female intuition."

Just then the girls heard the crunch of tires on the gravel drive. Maura ran to the window and saw Kevin's gray Porsche pull into turnaround.

"He's here! And I'm not ready."

"Calm down," Jill said. "You look gorgeous. Put on some perfume, and you'll be set."

With this finishing touch, Maura grabbed her purse and hurried downstairs, Jill on her heels. Following the sound of voices to the kitchen, they entered to find Kevin chatting with Lorna, who was enjoying a coffee break after several hours of schooling green hunters.

Maura had to suppress a sigh at Kevin's

neat appearance. He was wearing well-fitted, light tan slacks and a silk shirt open at the collar so that a small portion of his dark-haired chest was exposed. His sunglasses were pushed up on his head over his thick, dark hair. When he saw Maura, he smiled widely.

"You look great, Maura."

Maura flushed, but Lorna Warren came to her rescue.

"That outfit really is becoming. It's so nice to see you girls out of jodhpurs and jeans. Your father's up from the City, Kevin?"

"For a few days."

"Give him and your mother my best."

"They said to say the same. Ready, Maura?"

"As ready as I'll ever be."

"Nice to see you, Mrs. Warren, Jill." Then they were out the back door, walking toward the Porsche.

"You do look beautiful." He leaned over and whispered in her ear.

"And you look pretty handsome."

"A compliment at last. Can my heart stand it?"

"Well, you know I don't want to give you too many because of that swelled head of yours."

He opened the car door and held it as she got in. "And here I thought I'd mended my ways."

He strode quickly around to the driver's side and climbed in. As they turned out of the drive onto the main road, he reached over and squeezed her hand.

"Still nervous?"

95

"Yes."

"Don't be. I've warned Mother and Dad to be on their best behavior."

Maura couldn't help but laugh.

Actually the lunch went much better than Maura had expected. Mr. and Mrs. DeAngelo were both warm, open people, who did their best to put her at ease. She soon lost the feeling of being on inspection and was free to relax and be herself.

They were served lunch on the patio by Mario, one of the servants who'd come to the States with Kevin's father. There was fresh fruit, lobster salad, lemonade, and a delicate pastry and cream dessert.

Maura found Kevin's father delightful—his old-world charm, the soft accent that flavored his speech, the good humor that brought his distinguished dark head back in a gust of laughter at some witty comment made by his wife. She could see so much of Kevin in him—of him in Kevin.

Mrs. DeAngelo almost immediately brought up the subject of horses. "I understand from my son, Maura, that you're quite a rider."

"I try. I love it."

"You'll have to come over some day to have a look at my stables. Ever been up on an Irish hunter?"

"Ah, here we go again," her husband intoned, grinning widely, "another eulogy to the wonders of the Irish."

"You thought enough of them to marry one." She winked broadly to Kevin and Maura. "But to get back to our conversation, Maura. Have you—"

"No, though I've seen them work. There are several privately owned Irish hunters in the stable where I ride. They seem the strongest in the field, over a hunt course."

"Perceptive girl. Perhaps they lack the grace of thoroughbreds, but they have the stamina and heart to take you over anything."

"Now, Mother," Kevin interrupted, "you know Challenger and I were at the head of the field in both Virginia hunts."

"Oh, he has the speed, granted, but could you run him like that three, four days in a row? And how would he stand up to an Irish hunt?"

"Uno momento!" Mr. DeAngelo's voice interrupted what seemed to be a long-standing family argument. "I refuse once again to be a minority of one in a gathering of horse lovers. Tell me, Maura, have you been to Rome?"

"Yes, as a matter of fact I have." She grinned at his unsubtle changing of the subject. "But it was a long time ago, with my mother and father. I'd like to go back someday, though, to see it through older eyes."

"Yet surely you remember Saint Peter's, the Colosseum."

She nodded. "Though I didn't pay much attention to the history at the time. I only remember when we visited the Colosseum thinking how awful it was that the Christians had been fed to the lions."

"Today we are not so crude." He smiled. "We only feed them Irishwomen."

"Touché, Dad." Kevin laughed. "You got her that time."

"Touché, indeed. Your father will have crushed glass in his wine tonight."

"*Cara mia,* do not be so cruel. At least give me a quick, unsuffering death."

Mrs. DeAngelo's green eyes, so like her son's, flashed momentarily, then she, too, burst into laughter. "Some image we are presenting for Kevin's friend. Maura, please don't take this seriously. Normally we are a very loving family."

"I can see that, or you wouldn't joke so much. My parents have a way of teasing each other the same way."

"Tracey," said Mr. DeAngelo, rising, "why don't we leave the young people to their own pleasures."

"Yes, I think that's an excellent idea."

Mr. DeAngelo reached over and took Maura's hand. "It's been a pleasure meeting you, Maura. I hope we'll see you again."

"Thank you. I've enjoyed meeting you both."

Mrs. DeAngelo gave her a cheery smile. "Maura, I've always been a very unsubtle person. I like you. Come back. I'd enjoy riding with you."

"I'd enjoy that, too."

"Good. Now we oldsters will leave you alone. Have a nice time."

Kevin nodded.

"But come and say goodbye before you leave."

Chapter 13

"Was it so bad?" Kevin asked as his parents disappeared through the french doors.

"Not at all. I liked them."

"Good. They liked you, too."

"You could tell?"

"You bet," he assured her, smiling. "How about a walk?"

"Okay. Can we go through the garden first?"

"You like flowers?"

"Uh-huh. The garden seems to be something special."

"It is. My mother designed it after the gardens she remembered from staying with relatives in England and Ireland."

They entered a hedged enclosure full of marigolds, zinnias, dahlias, and summer roses in full bloom in manicured beds edged in low border flowers.

"Does she take care of all this herself?"

"Only the arrangement. A gardener comes in to do the actual work."

"It's like walking through the past when life was so much more leisurely."

"Do you really think so? Sometimes I do, too, and then wonder if I'm being too sentimental."

Kevin opened a wrought-iron gate leading out of the garden toward the pastures, and they wandered through. There were a few horses in the nearest meadow grazing peacefully.

"We alternate pastures," he explained. "Especially in a dry summer like this one when they tend to get overgrazed."

Following the white rail fences, they climbed the hillside toward the woods.

"It's cooler here," Kevin said as they finally stopped beneath the trees. They rested a moment, then resumed climbing the hill, which was quite high. Winded, they stopped again at a crest in a small clearing.

"It would be a lot easier on horseback," Kevin conceded.

Maura laughed. "We could have just stayed in the meadow."

"But this is someplace we've never been before. C'mon, let's go."

Kevin took her hand, and they slipped through the woods in the direction of the sound of a brook. When they found it, they discovered it was actually a small woodland waterfall with a pool beneath and a bit of grassy expanse of sunlit clearing to one side.

"Come on," Kevin called. "Let's go wading."

Though she'd traipsed across pastures and

climbed fences in her high heels and frothy skirt, Maura wasn't about to risk a soaking.

"Think again."

"I am thinking. Come on." Kevin had already removed his shoes and socks, and rolled up his slacks. "The water's fantastic, and you've got to be as warm as I am."

Maura hesitated, then finally took off her shoes and waded in. She had to admit the cooling waters felt good around her ankles, and the splash and ripples at the base of the small falls looked inviting. She only waded a few feet in, then Kevin unexpectedly grabbed her around the waist. She slipped and lost her footing. In the next instant, the two of them were sitting waist deep in the water.

"Oh, Kevin, look what you've done!" she shouted.

He was laughing too hard to say anything.

"How am I going to explain this to your parents?"

"Explain what?" He grinned. "Relax, Maura."

"Easy for you to say. It's so embarrassing!"

"What's the problem? The water's nice, isn't it?"

"It is," she admitted, "and I think I'm nuts, too!" She escaped from his arms and scrambled up onto the sunlit bank. She stood there trying to wring some of the wetness from her skirt. "What a mess!"

"It's all right," Kevin soothed. "Sit over there in the sun. You'll dry out in a second."

Flapping the material of her skirt so the air

would get at it, she turned and spied a soft bit of grass directly in the sun. Her back toward Kevin, she sat down, spreading her skirt around her. The sun was warm and she closed her eyes and lifted her face to its rays. She heard Kevin still splashing in the stream, but all else was peaceful, with only the whisper of the breeze in the treetops, the occasional call of a bird, the drone of a plane far in the distance. Feeling relaxed and lazy, Maura laid back on the grass and let her thoughts drift.

She was startled by cold droplets of water dripping on her face. Opening her eyes she saw Kevin standing over her. He had removed his shirt and was holding it over her. "I see, my woodland beauty, you're drying out, after all."

He moved away for a moment to spread his shirt on the grass, then returned to lie down beside her.

"Mind if I join you?"

"Not at all."

He lay back on the green carpet, one hand behind his head, his eyes closed. Maura had a quick glimpse of his broad chest and tautly muscled stomach before she, too, closed her eyes.

Kevin reached out his free hand and let his fingers rest gently against her arm. For a long while they were silent, dozing in the warmth, the trickling and splashing of the brook in the background.

Maura only half heard him as his voice spoke drowsily. "It's been a beautiful afternoon, don't you think?"

"Mmmm."

"The summer's almost over, Maura," he mused.

"I know. It's going too fast."

"I was thinking the same thing. I'm going to miss you in the fall."

"I'll miss you, too. It's been fun."

"Is that all it's been—fun?"

"Would you rather I said it's been terrible knowing you?" Maura chuckled and looked at him.

"I'm serious, Maura."

"Oh?" The tone of his voice made her uncomfortable. She didn't want to talk seriously—she didn't know how to handle it.

He paused before continuing. "I'd like to see you in the fall. It's only a two-hour drive from Harvard to Easton."

"But what about school?"

"Surely they give you weekends and vacations?"

"Yes...but I've never dated anyone. I don't know what my parents would say..."

"You're sixteen, Maura. You're growing up. Next year you'll be going away to college."

"I know. It's just that I never thought about it before. There's never been anyone I've *wanted* to date."

"Well, there is now, Maura."

Maura nodded. She didn't know what to say. She knew she cared about him, and she also knew she would miss him. But she didn't want to think about the fall.

Kevin rolled to his side and lifted himself

on one elbow. He stared down at her. "I want to see you—a lot of you." Sensing her reluctance to talk, he said, "but we can talk about it later, okay?"

She nodded again, inwardly breathing a sigh of relief.

"You make such a beautiful picture with your hair spread out on the grass." His fingers gently brushed the silky hairs away from her brow. He brushed his fingertips softly across her cheek, then down her neck. Maura felt an unexpected sensation, a mixture of delight and anxiety. Her heart was beating furiously.

"I'm going to hate the thought of all those miles between us," Kevin said. He leaned closer, then touched his mouth gently to hers. She closed her eyes, enjoying the sensation of his lips softly nibbling and kissing hers. Gradually his kiss grew strong and more demanding, and he pulled her close to him. She put her arms around him—she had never been kissed like this before.

Kevin's breathing became more rapid. He pulled his lips from hers for a moment and whispered hoarsely against her cheek, "Oh, Maura, Maura, I love you." His left hand moved from her back and gently touched her breast.

Maura stiffened. She wasn't ready for this. She had to stop him before he went any further.

"Kevin," she gasped, pushing his hand away, "stop...please stop."

"Maura," he rasped huskily. "I love you...I need you."

"I'm not ready! Please..."

He began kissing her again. She closed her mouth tightly and tried to turn her head away. His kiss became more forceful.

"Kevin, stop! Stop!" She brought her hands around to his bare chest, trying to push him away. But he wouldn't move.

This wasn't the Kevin she knew. What was he doing? Why wouldn't he listen to her? In desperation she slapped him soundly across the cheek.

His head jerked. His eyes snapped wide as he suddenly lifted them to look down at her frightened face.

"Let me go, Kevin!"

Unconsciously his arms loosened. She rolled away from him, scrambled to her feet, and stood, unable to control the sudden shaking in her body.

He remained on the grass, staring up at her as reaction slowly settled in. "Maura, I'm so sorry...please..."

"Why didn't you stop? I thought you cared about me!"

"I do. I care very much!" He was on his feet now, too, springing up in one smooth leap. "Please, Maura, listen to me."

"I want to go home. Now!" Even as she spoke, Maura sensed that the harshness of her tone was as much a result of her own fears as anger at him.

"Maura, I'm sorry," he pleaded. "Wait, let's discuss this."

"I don't want to talk, Kevin, please take me home. We'll talk tomorrow."

"This should be straightened out here and now. We're not children and when two people care about each other, they—"

"Tomorrow... we'll talk about it tomorrow."

He stared at her a moment silently. "All right. I'll get your shoes."

Their walk across the pastures was a somber one; the warm comraderie now was gone. Kevin tried once to reopen the subject and clear the air, but Maura rebuffed him. She was too uncertain of her own feelings to know what to say or whether to forgive him.

Their drive to the Warrens' was silent. He walked her to the door. "I'll see you tomorrow."

She nodded. "Tell your parents thank you again."

Chapter 14

That night Maura tossed and turned on her bed, reliving again in her mind the events of the afternoon. Her shock had gradually faded, replaced by a whirl of confusion. She had tripped so gaily along in her relationship with Kevin, always refusing to look at the future, the consequences of her actions. And now she was forced to.

He'd said he loved her. But what did that mean? The words had been said in a moment of passion; there was no way of knowing if he really meant it. Also he had told her that he found her a challenge; by telling her he loved her, he might have thought he could convince her to give in to him. The mere idea cut her to the core. She cared about him—and was finally realizing how much.

But even if he was being totally honest with her and did love her, was she emotionally prepared for the depth of the relationship he was proposing? Not just the physical part, which had brought her fears to the fore, but his plans for her—for them. Yes, she wanted to be with him, but she didn't want to tie herself steadily to one boy. There were so many things she wanted to do. She had her own career to plan— and her riding. Alex was talking of the National Horse Show. That would require a lot of work and total dedication. If only Kevin could leave it the way it had been—with the carefree friendship and the warmth of a relationship that put no serious demands on her.

She didn't want to lose him either, but it was just too sudden, too overwhelming for a girl who'd never before had any experience with love.

Maura woke from her restless sleep no closer to untangling her confusion than she'd been the night before. Her mind felt fuzzy and she was unable to concentrate. All she wanted to do was push it all away into the corner of her brain to be considered some day in the future when she was able to cope. If only she could put off meeting Kevin for a while. It was cowardly, she realized, but she just wasn't ready to talk to him.

Luck wasn't with her, however. As she was finishing her lesson, she heard the crunch of gravel and looked over to see Kevin's van.

He was waiting by the gate as she left the ring. When she saw the darkly determined look on his face, her heart sank. There would be no escaping a confrontation. She stiffened her spine and forced a courage she didn't feel.

He held the gate for her. "Good run," he said quietly.

"I didn't think you saw any of it."

"Just the end," he said.

"You're not riding this morning? Where's Challenger?"

"In the van. Maura, we were going to talk this morning."

"Yes," she said stiffly.

"Can I walk with you while you cool her out?"

"If you want."

He waited until they were a few yards from the ring, under the trees. "About yesterday, I wanted to apologize—"

"It's not necessary." She cut him off quickly.

"It is necessary. And why are you frowning?"

"I was just thinking."

"About what?"

"A lot of things."

"Yesterday," he said firmly.

Maura was torn by her desire to open up to him and her nagging fear that she could no longer trust him. "Yes," she finally replied.

"You're still angry."

"I'm just confused."

"I don't understand. Do you think differently of me now?"

"Yes...maybe...I don't know." She shook her head.

"Differently how?"

"The whole thing is different."

"Maura, I said I was sorry."

"And I said I accepted your apology."

"Then what's wrong?" At her silence he tried another approach. "Mother and Dad said to tell you how much they enjoyed meeting you."

"That was nice of them."

"They'd like you to come over Sunday. Mother's anxious to show you her hunters."

"Sunday?" Maura couldn't think that far ahead. "I don't know."

"Why are you being so cold?" Kevin asked, puzzled.

"Why can't we go back to the way we were before?" she suddenly burst out.

"What are you afraid of."

"I'm not afraid," she lied.

"You've got to grow up sometime, Maura—"

"For your information I *am* grown up and see and know a lot more than you think!"

"Well, you don't have to scream at me. Talk to me, for heaven's sake. Tell me what's bothering you."

"Nothing's bothering me! I just can't think, and you keep hammering at me—" With a stifled sob, she suddenly turned and ran off toward the stables, pulling Blackfire behind.

"Maura, wait!"

Ignoring his call, she disappeared inside the barn.

Kevin was about to follow when Alex came striding across the lawn, a concerned look on his face.

"Best to let her be, for the moment, I think. I didn't mean to eavesdrop." He cleared his throat. "A lovers' spat?"

His fists clenched at his sides, Kevin shook his head distractedly. He'd expected an entirely different greeting when he'd come to the farm that morning. "I don't know. She won't talk to me."

"Give her time. She has a lot on her mind with the show coming up."

"The show?" Kevin uttered, as though Alex were speaking of an entity from another planet.

"The horse show, remember?"

"Women!" Kevin muttered. "More and more I'm convinced we'd be better off without them!"

Alex laughed. "You're growing up, my boy. You've become initiated. Riding today?"

"Huh? Oh, yes—if I don't break my neck."

Which is precisely what Kevin seemed bent

110

on doing as he rode out his frustrations and anger. He pushed Challenger over the jumps at a hair-raising pace, clearing him over fences that would have made a professional cringe. Alex watched, wincing occasionally. It would do the boy good, he thought—Kevin needed an outlet. Perhaps it wouldn't hurt, though, to have a chat with Maura. No, he'd probably be putting his nose in where it didn't belong. He'd keep his silence.

The tension around Warren Farm was strong in the following days. Without deliberate intention Maura maintained her aloofness. Although she wanted to talk to Kevin, she had no idea what to say. She still wasn't certain of her own feelings. Sometimes she'd feel the words rising up in her throat, ready to be spoken, but she couldn't push them past the end of her tongue.

Kevin, on the other hand, continued to try to get through to her. Once he went out of his way to corner her in the barn, only to have her slip away with an excuse that she had to help Charlie. Another afternoon he arrived in his Porsche with the firm intent of taking her for a ride and talking, no matter what her excuse. But as he pulled into the drive, the Warrens' car was pulling out with Lorna and Maura inside. He motioned for them to stop, but apparently neither one saw his signal because the car continued on.

Unable to sort out the confusion in her mind, Maura put all of her energies into her riding, hoping somehow that the exercise and

111

exhaustion would put her into a drugged sleep at night and wipe out all thoughts of Kevin. Maura knew her behavior was turning Kevin away, and in her heart she didn't want to lose him, but she felt as if she were caught in a whirlpool that was dragging her along on its own course.

Now, instead of waiting around the farm in the afternoons, she'd go riding alone up into the hills or go swimming at the club. Jill, on the other hand, was happier than ever. Bill had finally come around to appreciate her and was spending more and more time with her.

The two of them had a date that Saturday night, and Maura spent a long, lonely evening in the bedroom listening to some sad songs on the stereo and feeling sorry for herself. By now she knew she was genuinely in love with Kevin—if the trembly, gut-gripping emotion she was experiencing could be called love. Still she was afraid to open up to him, afraid to believe that he genuinely loved her. At one point, she felt ready to declare her love to him, but at the last moment she backed off and retreated into the comparative safety of inaction. By admitting her love, she would at the same time be leaving herself open for hurt and rejection.

A few afternoons later she was swimming in the club pool when a dark head broke the surface of the water beside her. Black-lashed green eyes stared into hers.

"We're going to talk, Maura, even if I have to keep you out here in the middle of the pool the rest of the afternoon."

"Do you always scare the wits out of people like that, Kevin? And you make it sound as though we're enemies."

"In comparison to what we once were, yes."

"Don't be silly."

"I'm not. But you apparently are."

"In what way?" she said innocently.

"Maura, that won't work. I want to know what you're thinking and feeling."

She was silent. What could she say? She was no more ready than she had been a few days before.

"You know, Maura," Kevin began, "there was an afternoon not too long ago when we talked fairly seriously to each other. Now I feel like a leper."

"Don't."

"And?" His pride was such that he wasn't going to repeat his declaration of love to a girl who didn't seem willing to meet him halfway. He waited.

"And I'm sorry if I've seemed cool. I don't mean to be."

"Have your feelings changed?"

"Kevin, people are looking at us."

"I don't particularly care. They can stare if they want."

"Well, if you don't care, I do." She started to swim away. He came after her and halted her with a hand on her upper arm.

"Tell me one thing, Maura. If I asked you to go with me, would you?"

"No—I—" Before she could explain, his expression grew hard.

"That's all I wanted to hear. I'll be sure not to bother you in the future. Take care of yourself, Maura."

And he was gone, swimming swiftly away from her to the opposite side of the pool.

"Kevin..." but the word was barely a whisper from Maura's throat, and he didn't hear it. Without once looking back, he pulled himself from the pool and strode toward the parking lot.

Maura was too stunned to think clearly. In a moment she swam to the side of the pool, climbed out, found her towel, and lay down upon it. Only then could she allow herself to consider the words they'd just said to each other. He'd asked her to go with him. She'd refused. He'd said goodbye. She hadn't stopped him. Just like that it was over. She dropped her head down on her arms. The summer that had begun so beautifully had now turned into a disaster.

Chapter 15

Two days later Kevin showed up at the farm, late in the afternoon. Maura was home alone, up in the bedroom writing to her parents, whose last letter, sent from France, had arrived that afternoon. At the beginning of the summer, with all the excitement, Maura had thought about her parents very little. It was only recently that she realized how much she missed them. She wished that they would be here to see her ride in the show.

As she sat at the desk, her letter nearly completed, she looked out the window. A large van that she didn't recognize was pulling in. But she recognized the driver as he got out— and her heart started beating faster. It was Kevin. Why, she wondered, wasn't he driving his own one-horse van? A moment later Maura saw a girl with long, flaxen blonde hair emerge from the passenger side of the van and walk to the back to meet Kevin and help him open the doors. As the girl threw back her head, sweeping her long hair over her shoulder, Maura felt her heart wrench. The girl looked older—perhaps twenty—sophisticated, and seemed totally at ease with Kevin. She stepped back as Kevin disappeared into the van to get Challenger. He handed the reins to the waiting girl, went into the van again, and led out a bay. So that was why he needed the large van.

Maura watched as the two led their mounts to the ring, pausing once to tighten the girths and adjust the stirrups. Kevin gave the blonde a leg up. She laughed at something he said. Then he was up on his own saddle. Maura heard a few scattered words of their conversation.

"You're sure you're up to this?" he questioned pleasantly. "I know you haven't ridden in a while, but Chips is an easy goer. Stay to the rail if you want."

"I'd rather stay with you," she responded. "And it hasn't been all *that* long."

He laughed. "Well, just stay away from the tricky fences. I'm training for competition, and you're not."

"That's okay, I'd rather watch you, anyway." Her grin was dazzling.

Maura couldn't stand any more. As much as she wanted to see how well the lady rode, her heart couldn't take it. Quickly she pulled on her riding boots, went out to the barn, and saddled Blackfire. "We're going for a ride, girl," she said. "No matter what Alex thinks."

She let herself into the pasture behind the barn and walked Blackfire to the far side away from the ring. Blackfire seemed ready to go, so Maura put her to a canter, around and around the short grass, but it wasn't nearly enough to release Maura's anger. "Let's get out of here, girl—forget the gates."

Maura heeled Blackfire toward the three-rail pasture fence. She knew Alex would have had a fit if he knew she was jumping the mare over the fences that were supposed to be her boundaries, but she no longer cared. Also, she didn't stop to think that the pasture she was crossing was directly behind the riding ring and that when she sailed over the fence, she was in full view of the one person she was trying to avoid.

Maura and Blackfire went over the fence in a magnificent leap. She encouraged Blackfire on, across the next acre. They jumped the second fence. The farm seemed far behind as they worked their way up toward the hills.

Let him have his fun, Maura cried to herself. What did she care—except that it broke her heart.

Maura rode all the way to Kevin's meadow before she stopped. Blackfire was lathered; in her anger Maura had been pushing her. She walked the mare now, letting her nibble at the grass. Feeling only a dull ache in the area of her stomach, Maura wanted to cry, but the tears of release wouldn't come. He was with another girl, and she was alone. But it's your own fault, she kept telling herself.

Or was it? Was this actually a sign that she'd been right in doubting Kevin's sincerity? It didn't take him long to find another, she reasoned. Maura sighed deeply, the hurt tearing her apart. Well, at least there was the show to look forward to—that was her only consolation. And after what she'd seen today, she'd beat him—she'd beat the pride out of him!

When Maura returned to the farm, Kevin's van was gone. She was glad she wouldn't be tortured again by the sight of him and his blonde. Then why did she feel as though she'd missed something? Why did she feel so empty?

She saw Kevin at the farm the next morning, but again she deliberately ignored him. To have given him any kind of a welcome after what she'd witnessed the day before would have been more than she could bear.

Although Maura could never have guessed,

Kevin had been having second thoughts. At home in his room the night before, he'd realized just how foolishly he was behaving. He was still angry and hurt that Maura gave him no encouragement, but he knew in his heart he didn't want it to end. Bringing Justine, a fashion model he had nothing in common with, to the ring and flaunting her in front of Maura could only push them further apart, he realized.

Now, when he saw Maura disappear through the broken gate into the overgrown apple orchard, he tied Challenger to a rail and walked after her. Maura glanced back over her shoulder, saw him approaching, and immediately set off at a job trot. Knowing pursuit was hopeless, Kevin returned to the ring and loosened Challenger's reins. Never had he felt anything to compare to the humiliation and pain he was experiencing at that moment. Out of the corner of his eye a half hour later, he saw Maura return from the orchard, saw her pause a moment on the lawn watching him. He nearly lost stride but pulled himself together. And when he looked again a few moments later, she was gone.

At the pool the next afternoon, Kevin was with the same brunette. Maura saw them splash into the water together; noticed, too, that Kevin looked in her direction—a brief, fleeting glance. She felt an urge to dive into the pool, surface beside his sleek body, smile at his dark-haired friend, and tell her Kevin was already taken.

Clenching her fingers on her towel, she

listened abstractedly to the conversations going on around her. As Kevin hoisted himself from the pool, his eyes stared directly at Maura, and before she could pull her own away, he lifted his hand to her in a flamboyant salute, twisting the blade. Then he turned, dropped his arm around Justine's tanned, slender shoulders, and leaned his head down to say something in her ear. Justine laughed and flung back her head.

Maura's eyes followed them around the edge of the pool and into the parking lot. His Porsche was under the trees in clear view. He opened the door for Justine, then went around to his own side. His smile didn't seem as carefree now, but before that could register in Maura's mind, he'd climbed into the driver's seat, his expression hidden from her view. A few seconds later the car engine roared to life. Kevin backed out, swung around, then the car went up the drive and out of view.

In an effort to push her pain away, Maura concentrated more and more on her riding. She didn't need Kevin, she rationalized. She'd gotten along very well before meeting him and would get along without him very well now. The only problem was—she felt miserable.

Finally Jill, tired of her friend's moping face, confronted her.

"You may be my best buddy, Maura Langdon, but enough is enough. Why won't you talk to me?"

"About what?"

"You and Kevin, dummy. You stop seeing

him, and every time I ask you about it, you clam up. Why won't you tell me why you're running from him, turning him off? What terrible thing did he do?"

"You've seen him with his new friend."

"That's your fault. He didn't start running around with Justine until he got sick of getting the cold shoulder from you."

"Well, I can't stand to see the two of them together."

"Then do something about it," Jill said.

"Do what?" Maura blinked away the tears that had begun to fill her eyes.

"I'm sorry. I didn't mean to jump all over you. But from what I can tell, this all started right after you went to see Kevin's parents. Did they give you a hard time?"

"No, Kevin said they liked me."

"Then it was something else. Look, I don't mean to pry, Maura, but you've got to talk to someone."

Maura's voice quavered, but finally she forced out the words. "Kevin tried to get serious with me. Oh, he stopped, but not until I slapped his face. You see, he told me he loved me, but he'd never said it before then, and I was afraid he'd only said it so I'd do what he wanted."

"Did he apologize?"

"Yes, but I wasn't sure what to think. He said he wanted to see me in the fall, too, but—oh, I don't know, Jill, everything was happening much too fast. I couldn't talk to him then—I needed time to sort it all out."

"So you avoided him."

"I didn't mean it to seem that way—I just couldn't answer his questions. I didn't know *what* I felt."

"It's not too late."

"He has Justine, which more or less confirms that he wasn't being honest with me from the beginning."

"Don't you know anything?" Jill's voice was rising. "He's only using her to get back at you. It's obvious to me he cares about you. Try to explain to him how you feel."

Maura shook her head. "I still don't know what I want, so what can I tell him."

"The truth. If he cares at all for you, he'll understand. Besides, there's nothing wrong with not knowing what you want. It happens to everyone."

"I can't go to him now—not after Justine. I'll look like I'm begging."

"No, only making amends. After all, you started this."

"It's not all *my* fault, and I'm not going to let him see how much he hurt me."

"Listen to you—you sound like a little kid. Please, Maura, talk to him. Telling him how you feel couldn't make things any worse."

Maura shook her head stubbornly.

Jill threw up her hands in exasperation. "I don't know what to do with you. You're hopeless!"

Flipping over on her stomach, Maura pretended to be absorbed in the book that was open before her. Maybe Jill was right. Maura could see her point, but she wasn't going to risk making a fool of herself.

Although Maura continued to see Kevin almost every day, she never approached him. Occasionally, he'd bring Justine to the farm, and she'd stand at the rails, calling out encouragement.

Maura's heart hardened; her determination to beat him increased with each day that passed. She rode with such single-mindedness during her lessons that several times Alex had to tell her to back off and relax. He knew the reason behind Maura's relentless quest for perfection, but he didn't want Blackfire pushed too hard or else she'd turn into a bundle of nerves, too. One uptight lady was all he could handle at the moment.

Chapter 16

Maura began counting the days until the show, marking each one off with a black X on the calendar. She spent long hours alone, walking up across the fields, through the woods, sitting in the sunlight high in the hills, staring out over the rolling landscape. If only there was something in her heart to match that beauty. In a few weeks summer would be over, and it would be back to Easton, back to Maryvale. The thought left her cold. Kevin would go off to Harvard, and she'd probably never see him again. She sighed and blinked unexpected tears from her eyes. It was just as well—he probably never really loved her anyway.

Funny how much her opinions of him had changed in a few short months. She grinned wryly when she remembered what an arrogant snob she'd thought him in the beginning. How sure she'd been then; sure of who she was, what she wanted, positive she had full control over her emotions. And now she was sure of nothing—only that she ached for a return to that warm, understanding relationship Kevin and she had shared briefly.

Jill realized Maura had to work her problems out on her own. Nevertheless, she did what she could to cheer up her friend, inviting Maura out with Bill and her when they went to Danbury for a movie, twisting Maura's arm to come play a few sets of tennis at the club on a sunny afternoon. More often than not, however, Maura refused to join them. She felt uncomfortable being the third wheel, and at the club there was always the chance she'd run into Kevin with his new girlfriend.

The approaching two-day show brought on a frenetic burst of activity around Warren Farm. Both Lorna and Alex were preoccupied with the preparations. The flat pasture alongside the drive was roped off for parking. The fencing around the show ring was repainted, jumps repaired and refurbished. From mid-August on, trucks arrived on an almost daily basis with new equipment, including a long flatbed of bleachers, which would be assembled on three sides of the ring. The turf of the ring was regraded and raked to a fine powder, and all stones larger than the size of a pebble were removed. In the large, grassy pasture behind the ring, jumps were readied for the open hunt competitions.

Alex rushed around all over the farm, supervising workmen, giving instructions to Charlie to see that the extra stalls were immaculate, extra feed supplies brought in, liniment and bandages in stock. He had the traveling blacksmith up to reshoe and repair.

Lorna Warren was busy arranging for the refreshments and conveniences for the expected crowd. Two stands would be set up on the lawns to provide cold drinks and quick food. There would be several overnight guests, too, close friends of the Warrens who would be coming from some distance. Cara was busy cleaning the guest rooms and putting fresh linen on the beds, preparing ahead for the dinner party the first evening, the morning breakfast.

Jill had decided not to compete after all, but she was more than happy to join Maura in the tack room, rubbing down saddles and bridles with saddle soap.

Despite the fact they were acting as hosts, the Warrens would both be competing—Mrs. Warren in an open hunter event; Mr. Warren in the adult dressage class; and in between all the activity, time still had to be found for practice. While the main ring was being graded, Maura used the smaller ring, where Alex had temporarily set up a series of jumps. By the time of the show, this ring would be cleared for use as a warm-up area. Alex continued his coaching when he could spare the time, but more often than not, he left Maura on her own. He had total confidence in her now.

Maura knew Kevin was pushing as hard as she was, often practicing at Maple Park now because of the confusion at Warren Farm. The winning of the blue ribbon had become a personal confrontation between them, a battle of pride between two strong-willed people. It was no longer a matter of personal satisfaction—now Maura *had* to win.

The afternoon before the show, the first horse vans began arriving at the farm, pulling into the roped-off pasture in a steady procession. Most of these early arrivals were old friends and acquaintances of the Warrens. Maura and Jill were on hand to greet them and joined Lorna and her friends in the kitchen for coffee and refreshments. Maura couldn't get over all the activity; she was introduced to more people that afternoon than she could remember.

The following morning, however, would be even busier. The initial events were scheduled to begin at ten, and most of the participants, together with the spectators, would arrive in the three hours preceding. Maura was so nervous she could barely function. All she could think was that she'd soon be facing Kevin. But every available hand was needed to help with preparations, and Jill and Maura were soon pressed into service. In the kitchen they helped Cara and the extra staff brought in for the occasion. They lent a hand to Charlie in the stables, feeding and watering the Warrens' stock. They ushered the overnight guests to their rooms and saw that they had everything they needed. Later, they directed the caterer's truck to the kitchen entrance and the concessionaires to the areas on the lawn set aside for their stands.

There was no sign of Alex except a fleeting glimpse here and there as he bustled between the ring and the hung field, issuing orders, pacing out distances between the jumps that were to be erected. In the parking area, there was also a lot of activity. Vans were situated, horses brought out into the sunlight to stretch their legs. Some were stabled in the Warrens' barn; others let out into one of the paddocks. The owners and riders milled about, talking, sharing refreshments, checking and cleaning tack, comparing notes on events in which they would be competing, discussing places where they might go to get an evening meal.

The Warrens' closest friends would be having dinner in the house, and Maura understood there would be fourteen seated around the large dining room table. She welcomed all the activity, since it gave her little time to think of her own worries. It was Lorna who had her sympathy at the moment. The poor woman was

126

at her wit's end, trying to divide her time between her guests and the preparations.

Finally things quieted down a bit just before dinner, and Jill and Maura went to their room to shower and change.

"Excited, Maura?" Jill questioned. "I can't believe it's here. I really never expected it to be this big."

"Neither did I. I only hope my nerves hold out."

"Early to bed for you tonight. What time's your first event?"

"Not until one. But that's only hunters over fences. Sunday's the big event."

"Kevin riding tomorrow? Or shouldn't I ask?"

"I think he is, though he'll be competing out in the field, thank God."

Jill frowned. "You're more nervous about facing him than all the spectators."

"I don't even want to think about Kevin. I'm nervous enough as it is, but once I get in the ring, I should be all right—at least I always have been before. Is Bill coming?"

"You bet your life."

"The sacrifices one makes for love," Maura teased, knowing Bill's lack of enthusiasm for horses.

"Oh, don't go feeling sorry for him. He may not like riding, but he enjoys watching."

"It's a shame you decided not to ride."

"Are you kidding? With that crowd out there? It's the best decision I ever made."

Maura laughed. "I hope your pessimism doesn't rub off on me."

127

"Never happen—you wouldn't give up this chance for a million dollars. Right?"

"Right."

"Besides we'll all be there to cheer you on."

Dinner was pleasant. Maura was particularly caught up with all the horse talk. Several of the Warrens' friends were up from the Virginia hunt country, an entirely new world to Maura, who soaked up their descriptions of the countryside and praise of the hunt. She was fascinated, too, by the gossip—what events were scheduled for the fall season, the entertainments planned, who had bought whose hunter. Maura knew Kevin and his mother had gone down for the hunt season the year before and wondered if they'd be going down again. The people at the table probably knew him, though she didn't have the courage to ask.

The conversation eventually swung around to the show, and they compared notes.

"You know I'm only riding for the fun of it," one fair-haired lady admitted. "I lost the competitive spirit years ago, but I have to get Jingles out in front of a crowd occasionally to show him he's still wanted."

There were answering chuckles.

"So tell us, Alex," Rodney Talmadge, a deep voiced, ruddy-faced Virginian called out. "What tricks have you got in store?"

"My lips are sealed. Everything you need to know will be in the programs distributed tomorrow."

"Just thought I might surprise you into a slip or two."

"Never fear. What we have in store will live up to your expectations."

"Sly devil. Not doing any open jumping yourself this year, Alex?"

"No, only dressage. I have enough on my hands, although the farm will be represented."

"By Lorna?"

"Yes—and another."

"More secrets?"

To Maura's relief, Alex left it a mystery. "You'll see tomorrow. More particularly on Sunday."

As the adults sat over their coffee, Maura and Jill excused themselves and went to the kitchen to see if they could help Cara. That efficient woman had things well in control, but realizing the girls were high-strung with excitement and needed something to keep them occupied, she handed them each a dish towel and set them to work drying the fine crystal glasses that had been hand washed.

Nearly an hour later, Alex wandered into the room.

"Everything all right, Mr. Warren?" Cara inquired a bit nervously.

"Magnificent. As usual you've done an excellent job. The party's breaking up now—everyone needs an early night. I just thought I'd stop in here to see if you needed any help. I don't want you up all night."

"We were just finishing up, as a matter of fact. Jill and Maura were giving me a hand."

"Good girls—" he smiled appreciatively—"though it's time you thought of bed yourselves."

"Maura's not going to sleep," Jill commented, "until she's so exhausted she passes out on the bed."

Alex, concerned, looked to his houseguest. "Nervous?"

"A little."

"Normal preshow jitters. If you weren't nervous, then I'd be worried. You're going to do fine—just fine."

"After listening to them talk at dinner," Maura admitted, "I feel outclassed. This is my first heavy competition."

"And no one will guess. My friends may live and breathe horses, but there's not a serious professional among them—not that there won't be a few serious riders here Sunday. They'll give you a run for your money, but I don't see that you'll have anything to worry about. Actually your stiffest competition is going to come from right here in the neighborhood."

"Kevin."

He nodded. "The boy's good, and he's got a rod of determination for a spine."

That was the last thing Maura needed to hear. Realizing his mistake, Alex reached out and patted her shoulder.

They were interrupted by Lorna, who came bursting into the kitchen. "Oh, Alex," she cried, running over. "I just had the most horrible thought. The ribbons. I don't remember where I put them! I thought they were in the study, but I went to check and—"

"Lorna, my dear, will you relax!" He put an arm around his wife's shoulders. "I brought them to the judges yesterday so they could put them in order. I guess I forgot to tell you." His look was sheepish.

"Thank goodness! All I could think was I'd lost them—and what is a show without ribbons?"

"You've got too much on your mind, sweetheart. I'm beginning to think perhaps we overextended ourselves hosting this event."

"No, never." She looked up at him, her face tired but her eyes bright. "I know how much it means to you. I just want it to be perfect."

"And so it shall. Now, as I've told the girls, I think it's time for bed—you're completely exhausted."

"I won't argue with you there."

"Our guests all right?"

"Yes. The Parkers and Meisens are still in the living room, but I'm sure they won't mind if we go up before them."

"We'll just say good night to them, then." His arm still about her shoulders, he led her away. Then with a backward glance to the girls, he said, "And you two scat. Up to bed."

"Good night," Jill and Maura chorused.

"Sleep well."

Chapter 17

Saturday morning Maura and Jill were jerked awake by the sound of the screaming alarm clock. As the dawn glow filtered through the curtains, the sound of chirping birds and activity downstairs drifted in the open windows.

"Oh," groaned Jill, stretching, "am I really getting up at five-thirty? I must be insane."

"How can you be a lazy bones on today of all days?" Maura said, astonished. Wide awake, she was already out of bed, pushing her long, sleep-mussed hair from her eyes and grabbing her robe.

"You know my blood doesn't start circulating until at least nine o'clock."

"Well, you can begin the motions while I go in and take a shower—a quick one, I promise."

"Thank goodness that with all these guests there're four bathrooms."

"That won't mean much if the water runs out," Maura joked.

"Uncle Alex must have thought of that before he invited all these people."

"See you in a minute. Out of bed, sleepy-head, or I'll gladly pull you out."

Jill grimaced and stuck out her tongue at her well-meaning friend, but Maura was already disappearing out the door.

Only Lorna and Alex Warren were up when Jill and Maura entered the kitchen. Cara was busily setting out a buffet breakfast on the long harvest table. The guests would be invited to help themselves, then find a spot outside on the lawn to eat.

"Good morning," Alex called out. "Glad to see you up and about. We'll need a jump on the rest of the crew here. Fill your plates."

A little while later, a few other early risers began straggling down. In the yard there was the sound of wheels on gravel, and a big four-horse van pulled in, followed the arrows, and turned into the pasture.

"Well, it's started," Alex Warren said, more to himself than anyone else, a stifled jubilance in his voice. Then he turned seriously to the members of his family group. "Before things get too hectic, let me have a word with you all. Jill, your aunt will need help today."

"We've already made arrangements." Jill grinned.

"Fine. Now, Lorna, I don't want you wearing yourself out. Everything's been planned down to a fine point and should pretty much take care of itself. You'll be riding in the ten o'clock hunter class—no more nervous frazzles like yesterday."

"After a good night's sleep, I feel like a new woman."

He winked at her. "Now for Maura, our champion. Help out if you want—probably a good idea for you to be busy to ward off the jitters—but take it easy. I want to see you in the stable at one sharp. Get Blackfire out and walk her a bit, then warm her in the small ring. Nothing dramatic, just get her limbered. Today will be our testing ground. Neither of you should have a thing to worry about. I've put you in this hunter class to get you both used to the crowds, give them a taste of what's in store for them tomorrow. Feeling all right?"

"I feel great! Nervous, but great."

"Fine. I've got to get going. But I'll be there when you're riding, my dear." He dropped a quick kiss on his wife's cheek.

The rest of the morning went quickly for Maura. For a while she helped Jill bundle programs and bring them to the admissions booth that had been set up at the end of the drive. By then a steady stream of vans and trailers belonging to competitors was pulling in. It was too early for the spectator crowd, though some had come early in order to get good seats.

Unconsciously Maura kept watching for the DeAngelo van. Finally, at eight-thirty, she was rewarded. Kevin was driving, with Mr. and Mrs. DeAngelo on the front seat beside him. When the elder De Angelo spied her standing on the lawn near the drive, they both gave a happy wave. Maura returned their greetings—her quarrel wasn't with them. The van was lost from sight as it followed others into the parking area, and Maura had things to do. She'd promised Charlie she'd give him a hand at the stables keeping unwanted visitors out, and she wanted to check Blackfire. The mare had been vigorously groomed the day before, but Maura wanted to be sure the sleek, ebony satin coat gleamed.

The mare could sense the excitement. She needed attention and a soothing hand. Maura gathered up a brush and comb and put Blackfire in crossties near the one open stable door.

"Well, girl," she said softly as the mare nickered to her, "it's almost time. Yes, you're excited, I can see that. Let's just polish you up." Maura brought the brush over the gleaming hide. The muscles in Blackfire's back rippled in pleasure. "I probably should braid your mane and tail—looks more stylish, you know." Maura giggled. The mare seemed to understand, rubbing her chin on Maura's arm. "Personally I think you look flashier with your hair blowing in the wind, but maybe just two small braids at the top and bottom, tied with red ribbon." Maura set to work with her comb, braiding the satin ribbon into the strands of hair, trying not to think of the upcoming events—and Kevin. She stood back when finished to inspect her work. "Not bad. And now maybe just a touch at the top of your tail."

Maura tied off the ends of the ribbon she'd cross-laced around the upper end of Blackfire's long, luxuriant tail, then gave the mare's rump a pat. "Well, I think we're ready, old girl." Feeding the mare a carrot, she released her from the crossties and led her to her stall. "I'll be back at one."

The crowd on the lawns had grown three-fold by the time Maura left the barn. She shook her head in amazement as she waded through the bodies. It was nearly ten—time for the first class to begin. Already riders were warming up in the small ring, while jumps were checked and repositioned in the field. Courses would be periodically changed during the day for different events. Only for the open jumping competition on the following day was the ultimate course kept a mystery.

Lorna Warren's class was coming up in the field, and Maura pushed in that direction. As she hurried around one of the refreshment stands making for the back pasture, paying little attention to where she was going, she nearly collided with Mr. DeAngelo. But he saw her coming and quickly backed out of the way.

"Well, Maura," he said in his accented tones, "so good to see you again, if a little precipitously."

"Hello, Mr. DeAngelo," Maura answered. "Yes, I was in kind of a hurry. Sorry for the near accident."

"With this crowd it's to be expected. I understand from my son you'll be riding today."

"Yes. This afternoon."

"Good luck."

"Thanks. Both your wife and son are riding, too?"

"But, of course. They wouldn't miss it for

the world. As a matter of fact, my wife will be riding in a few minutes in the back field."

"Then she must be in the same class as Mrs. Warren."

"No doubt. Lorna and Tracey often compete together. I was looking for the Warrens earlier, but couldn't find them anywhere."

"They're here...both very busy."

"I can imagine. Were you on your way to see Lorna ride? I'll walk with you, if you don't mind."

"Not at all."

As they strolled through the crowd, Mr. DeAngelo spoke as though thinking aloud. "My son has seemed so preoccupied lately. I hope it doesn't affect his riding."

"He's done excellently the times I've seen him practice." Maura fought to keep her tone nonchalant.

"Mmm, you're a better judge than I. From what Kevin's told me in the past, he has great hopes for these competitions."

Maura was silent. There was nothing she could say.

"My wife and I so enjoyed having you to lunch. I don't wish to pry into what has happened between you and my son. Let me only say that we hope to see you again at Maple Park."

Maura was touched by his words. "I hope so, too."

He smiled gently. "I see Kevin waiting over there at the fence. Would you like to join us?"

"No—that is, thank you very much, but I have a friend waiting." Maura motioned in the opposite direction toward Jill, who had her arm raised to catch Maura's attention.

He extended his hand, and Maura grasped it. "Then let me again wish you much luck."

"Thank you. Nice to see you, Mr. DeAngelo."

Each turned in separate directions, but not before Maura had caught the frown Kevin directed toward them. She abruptly turned away from his gaze.

"Did I see what I think I saw?" Jill exclaimed, wide-eyed, as Maura reached her side.

"Yep, that was Mr. DeAngelo."

"What did he say? And did you see Kevin practically popping his eyeballs watching the two of you?"

"How could I miss it? As for Mr. DeAngelo, he was only being pleasant. I sort of ran into him—physically—coming from the stables to get here in time."

"That's all?" Jill asked disbelievingly.

"We'll talk about it later. I see Mrs. DeAngelo is coming into the field."

Jill glanced up with interest. "I've heard she's good—the one Aunt Lorna's going to have to beat."

The tall, auburn-haired woman was coming around toward the first fence on one of her big Irish hunters. It was an interesting course —something Maura had never seen before— with the jumps set out over an unusually long distance. It was reminiscent of a hunt field in miniature, in the shape of an elongated horseshoe. A difficult event to judge because of the distance involved, and to compensate, an extra judge had been stationed at the far side of the field.

Although she'd been offered the opportunity to come to Maple Park on Mrs. DeAngelo's invitation, Maura had never seen Kevin's mother ride before. The Irish hunter she was riding was strong, yet for all his big-boned strength, they cleared the first fence gracefully. It wasn't difficult to see that this horse was a champion. He wasn't remotely winded when they finished with a clean round. There was a burst of applause, which continued until the next rider appeared on the course.

The second contestant didn't fare as well, misjudging her fifth fence, getting a refusal, trying again, and finally sending her mount over. But the fault had cost her valuable points.

Mrs. Warren was third from last in the field, coming out on one of her prize long-legged, clean-limbed hunters. Maura had seen her training the gelding many times. He was a gray five-year-old, bred on the farm, an excellent jumper who put his heart into it, but who was still green.

Mr. Warren came up behind Jill and Maura, and as his wife began, he lifted his arm in salute. Lorna caught the gesture out of the corner of her eye, then put her mind to it.

Her gelding was game, prancing into a canter until Lorna smoothly evened his pace. Unlike Mrs. DeAngelo's more muscular mount, the gray was pure poetry as he leaped over the barriers. The test was whether he could finish the second half of the course with as much ease.

"Easy now. Don't rush him," Alex said under his breath. "Good, nice pace. Keep it smooth."

Jill jabbed her uncle's ribs.

He laughed. "An extra bit of encouragement."

Apparently his wife didn't need it, because she came through beautifully with a clean round. There was a loud burst of applause.

Alex crowed in victory. "She's done it! I didn't want to get her hopes up too high, girls, but what do you say?"

"There's only Mrs. DeAngelo and the man on the ginger gelding to beat her."

They waited impatiently as the last riders had their turns. Then the judge from the top of the field strode down to consult with his fellows on the stand. The microphone squawked to life.

"Ladies and gentlemen, your attention. The winners for the first event." The speaker consulted the pad before him. "In fourth, Mr. Thomas Ward on Spirit of Ridgewood Stables. Cheshire, Connecticut. Third, Mr. James Krensky on Willows, privately owned, of Salem, New York." The announcer paused, knowing the crowd's anticipation. "In second, and fine ride, Mrs. Ricardo DeAngelo on Irish Mist of Maple Park, Southbury, Connecticut." A cheer went up from the gathering as Tracey DeAngelo came forward, her smile wide. This was her first event. She had three more classes in which to compete and try for a blue.

"And now in first, for the blue ribbon, Mrs. Alex Warren on Smokey of Warren Farm, Southbury, Connecticut."

Alex gave both Maura and Jill bear hugs. "She won! She'll be so happy! I'm so proud of her!"

"We are, too, you know, Uncle Alex."

"She deserved it," Maura added.

"What are we waiting for? Let's go congratulate her!" He took them by their elbows and hurried them along the fence. The DeAngelos had already surrounded their ribbon winner and were pulling her off, away from the crowd. Maura cast one longing look in that direction, then remembered herself.

Lorna's cheeks were flushed with victory as her husband reached her side, threw his arms about her, and gave her a smacking kiss. Maura and Jill couldn't hear the words that passed between them, but when they lifted their heads, both were laughing.

"Aunt Lorna," Jill cried, giving her a hug, "you were fantastic!"

"Congratulations!" Maura echoed.

"Thanks. I'm still heady. I had no idea I'd take the ribbon. I'm just so excited!" She was like a young girl again, exhilarated, giggling. "Oh, Alex, you should have entered some of the hunter events, instead of that dry old dressage."

"Perhaps, but then I can only concentrate my energies in so many directions, and who's to say I'd do as well as you, my dear?"

"But look how well you've coached me," Maura exclaimed. "You must be a fantastic rider."

"Not necessarily. It's one thing to tell a good rider what they're doing wrong and how

141

to correct it—another to mount up and do the same thing myself. There are those meant to be teachers, and those meant to be doers. You fall into the latter category."

Maura's cheeks flushed with the compliment.

The few hours until Maura's event passed quickly. At twelve she went up to get into her dress outfit: beige, tight fitting jodphurs, white shirt, white stock, dark blue jacket, and gleaming black hunt boots. She drew her long hair back into a bun at her neck, set in place her black velvet hard hat. There was an under-the-chin strap that she would secure later. Taking a last look at herself in the mirror, she felt ready.

She was at Blackfire's stall promptly at one. Alex strolled in a few minutes later.

"I knew you'd be ready." He smiled. "Now there's nothing to worry about. You and this lady will breeze through. Just relax and do what you've been doing these last weeks in practice. You'll get your number outside the main gate."

"I won't forget."

"I'll be at ringside, but I can't encourage you, can't coach. You'll be on your own."

"I know."

"Go to it, girl."

Blackfire was anxious and stomping in her stall. The mare's ears perked as Maura brought her out. Maura stopped to get her lightweight cardboard number and fastened it to her back. She then went out to the warm-up ring. As she passed, Maura checked out the positioning of fences in the huge main ring and found a semicircular round of medium difficulty. As Mr. Warren had said, this would be a testing ground.

Maura's number was called seventh. Though somewhat nervous as she entered the ring, in that special way of hers, she blocked the outside world from her mind. The crowd no longer seemed so loud. She could feel Blackfire's emotions through her hands and her knees. As the mare pranced excitedly, Maura leaned forward and whispered in her ear, "Easy girl. Let's ride like we've always done."

Blackfire calmed down, her ears flicking back. She felt the knees, the hands on the reins.

"Let's go, girl." Maura circled at the end of the ring. Blackfire's paces were smooth. Occasionally she rolled her eyes in the direction of the crowd, but Maura soothed her.

Maura dug her heels into the stirrups and gripped her knees. "Now, girl." Because of the mare's excitement, Maura sat her canter almost to the first jump. They sailed over.

After the second fence, Maura breathed a sigh of relief. Blackfire and she were together. Everything was perfect. The mare had forgotten her nervousness and was jumping with her whole heart, as was her nature. At the fifth fence, a double rail, the most difficult on the course, Maura checked Blackfire's ongoing stride, then heeled her into a superlative leap that cleared the rails with almost a foot to spare.

Although the crowd cheered as she came off, Maura was unaware as she mentally tried to judge her own performance. Alex met her as she left the gate. "I think you've taken it."

"Taken what?"

"The blue in this event!"

"Are you sure?"

"Let's watch what follows. There are still five riders behind you."

Even in her heady state, she could see that the competition didn't come close to matching what she felt she and Blackfire had done.

As one of the judges approached the microphone, Maura held her breath. Announcements were made for fourth, third, second.

"And in first place, Miss Maura Langdon on Blackfire of Warren Farm, Southbury, Connecticut."

Letting out her breath in a long sigh, Maura beamed to Alex as she trotted up to collect her ribbon. Amid the crowd on the far side of the ring, she saw Kevin watching her intently.

Maybe she'd given him something to worry about after all.

Chapter 18

With her win the previous day, Maura approached the open jumping competition on Sunday with a bit more confidence. She'd seen Kevin take a first in the men's hunter trials the previous afternoon, but even his excellent performance didn't shake her new assurance. Alex Warren had been right to have her ride in the hunter class; she was accustomed to the crowd now and knew for certain that she and Blackfire wouldn't fall apart under the eyes of the noisy spectators and professional riders present.

Only the most difficult events were scheduled for Sunday—ride-offs, advanced hunter trials, and the junior and advanced open jumping events. She and Kevin, along with ten other riders, would be competing in the latter. Their class was scheduled for one o'clock, the climax of the show, with the hunter trials being the last event.

On Alex's stern orders, Maura went up to her bedroom at eleven to rest, though she was so filled with anticipation that any real rest was impossible. She did lie on her bed for an hour, listening to the boisterous clamor outside her windows, the sound of the loudspeaker announcing events and winners.

At twelve, unable to lie still a moment longer, Maura rose, showered, did a few limbering exercises on the bedroom rug, then began dressing in her best attire.

When she reached the stables, Blackfire was outside her stall, saddled and waiting. Both Charlie and Alex were standing beside her.

"Ready to go, young woman? As you can see"—he patted the mare's neck—"this lady is all anticipation. Let me just run through the event quickly for you again. You'll go through the course once, being judged for faults. Those with clean rounds or highest scores will ride again with the fences raised, and so forth, until there is a clear winner. It could mean you might go through the course only once or as many as five or six times. Stamina will be important, so conserve her; keep her paced. I don't want her blowing herself out after the third round—she's excited to begin with. Any questions?"

Maura shook her head.

"Then good luck. We're all rooting for you. You'll have a small gleeclub waiting just to the left of the judges' stand. Warm her up in the small ring. The event should be called"—he checked his watch—"in about fifteen minutes. We're on schedule. You'll have a chance to check out the competition, but don't worry about them; just concentrate on your own performance. I've got to get back out there." He gave her a quick, fatherly hug. "You can do it."

"Thanks, Mr. Warren."

She turned to Blackfire and took the reins Charlie handed her as he tightened the girth. "Well, you're all set, miss. Good luck from me, too. I'll be out there watching." He winked. "Seen you jump, and I'll be putting my money on you."

"Ah, Charlie, that's sweet of you." Maura grinned and took the old man's extended hand. "I'll try not to disappoint you."

Maura, her number tied securely to her back, entered the warm-up ring, mounted, and set Blackfire off at a walk around the rail. There were about six other riders in the ring with her, none of whom she recognized. All were well mounted; there wasn't an animal under sixteen hands, though Blackfire was the only mare. The one rider she'd hoped to see, Kevin, wasn't there, which meant he was probably warming Challenger out in the paddock. Her fellow riders were too intent on their upcoming performances to spare any time for conversation, though Maura did receive a smile or two. Being the youngest one in the group, Maura was sure they considered her wet behind the ears and no real threat.

The loudspeaker blared. The winners for the previous event were announced. A scattering of applause could be heard for each of the ribbons awarded, but it seemed as if the audience, too, was waiting with baited breath for the open jumping, the most exciting event of them all.

There was a five-minute wait as the jumps for the course were rearranged and heightened and new obstacles were brought into the ring.

"And now, ladies and gentlemen, the advanced open jumping competition. Out first, number twenty-four, Mr. Willis Blake of Longacre Stables, Martinsville, Pennsylvania, on Summer Wind."

A man on a dappled gray rode up to the open gate and entered. Blackfire had had sufficient warm-up, and Maura decided she wanted to watch. She positioned herself so she could keep the mare at a walk and still see over the heads of the standing spectators. Mr. Blake was halfway through the course. With a quick glance, Maura checked the height and variation of the jumps. They were mixed, as she'd expected, higher difficulty with simple gates, a roll top, several brushes. The last fence would be the hardest. Three rail fences were set one behind the other with room for a stand of brush between each—a long, high jump.

From what Maura could estimate, the first rider was doing very well, but was that a clip she heard as he went over the last fence? She couldn't be sure, and by then the next rider was being called, one of the three women competing in the event. She didn't do as well, getting a refusal at the double brush, clipping one of the difficult rails. The horse was skittish, and so was the rider.

Another number was called, and another. Maura was becoming impatient. She continued to walk Blackfire. By now she'd gotten a comprehensive view of the course and felt sure she and the mare could handle it. But this waiting was driving her crazy—not to mention wondering where Kevin was.

Then her number was called. She leaned quickly over the mare's ear. "This is it, girl. Do your stuff."

In the few seconds from the time her number had been called, Maura's mind had already blocked out all extraneous details. She put Blackfire into a canter, coming around the top of the ring toward the first gate, sailing over, landing, and on to the second obstacle, a four-foot brush. Rider and horse were one body, clearing the brush, proceeding to the wall, then to the roll top. Maura carefully gauged Blackfire's pace for the approach to the half wall and double rail ahead, then on to another easy gate, the second brush. Then she approached the last triple fence. She collected Blackfire; her canter was sure and powerful. At the last second Maura squeezed hard. The mare flew, high and wide, Maura lifting forward over her neck, heels down, knees tight.

Perfect, a perfect round. Maura knew it even before she heard the loud burst of applause. Good. At least she had a chance against Kevin.

There were two more riders, then Kevin's number was called. Maura saw him approach quickly from behind her. He must have been waiting only a few yards away, checking the course as Maura had done earlier, but in her absorption, she hadn't been aware of his presence. As he passed he looked suddenly in her direction. Their eyes held for the briefest instant, then he nodded and continued through the gate that was being held open for him.

Maura felt suspended as she watched. Both horse and rider were in perfect form, eager, determined, totally together. Their timing was perfect; every fence was clean. What a beautiful run, Maura thought. By far the best performance yet. As Kevin brought Challenger away from the last fence, he smiled in appreciation of the crowd's cheer. He seemed confident as he left the ring, but Maura didn't have a chance to observe him too closely as the next competitor came trotting past her to the gate.

Finally the last rider came out of the ring. The judges huddled together as those of the entrants who felt they had even the smallest chance of continuing waited anxiously.

Then the announcement came. "With perfect scores for a run-off in a second round, number twenty-four, Willis Blake, number eighteen, Janis Vargas, number seventeen, Maura Langdon, number nine, Kevin DeAngelo."

There were cries of relief from the finalists, disappointed sighs from the others. Maura sat firm. She didn't look at Kevin to see his reaction, though she sensed he was sitting as unmovingly as she was.

The jumps were raised. Again they began pounding around the course. Janis Vargas was immediately eliminated with a knocked-down rail at the last fence. Then it was Maura's turn. Again she and Blackfire worked together to defy

150

everything around them. Kevin's run was also perfect, just as inspiring.

The loudspeaker boomed again. "With perfect scores for a run-off in a third round, number twenty-four, number seventeen, number nine."

Willis Blake set off and did magnificently but misjudged his last fence. His mount hesitated and clipped the last rail.

It was between Kevin and Maura.

Chapter 19

Maura entered the ring, making a quick mental assessment as she circled Blackfire. She would need stronger approaches and more collection with the higher fences. The mare was willing, eager, almost as fresh as she'd been for the first round. With Blackfire going in an easy canter, Maura organized herself, shoulders straight, head up, heels down, legs tight. She circled and approached in a hunt seat. Blackfire's ears perked forward intelligently as she spied the fence. This was the mare's natural element, and despite the workout she'd already received, she was anxious to try it again.

Round the course they went, mare and

rider. A hush had fallen over the crowd. They knew the importance of this ride. Should she complete the round without fault, it was up to Kevin to match her. If he did, they would face each other again in another run-off.

Maura was unaware of the hush. Concentrating only on her performance, she counted strides before the wall, gathered Blackfire for the leap over the double rail, squeezed, released. She was approaching the final fence that had been the undoing of the last contestant. She gathered Blackfire as they came around the turn, then faced her in. The mare knew what was expected of her. Her hindquarters churned, at the last moment releasing a huge burst of muscle power to send horse and rider into the air.

Maura brought the snorting, excited Blackfire into a circle to slow her, calm her.

There was a moment's silence, then sudden, spontaneous applause. "Bravo! Well done!" came the cries. Maura didn't dare let herself respond or relax—there might still be another round.

And in a moment Kevin proved he wasn't to be outdone. His eyes focused straight ahead, his expression hard, Kevin sent his spirited mount once again over the fences. Challenger moved as a leaping deer. Maura studied the stallion's every stride, his take off, his landing. She couldn't help but admire Kevin's firm control, the strength of his hands, the tautness of his legs, the ironlike resolution etched on his features. His round was faultless, and he came off the course to further cheers. The crowd was in ecstasy. Never had they expected such a display of skill as they were witnessing that afternoon.

"Two perfect rounds, ladies and gentlemen. For an additional run-off, number seventeen, Maura Langdon on Blackfire, and number nine, Kevin DeAngelo on Challenger."

This was it. Maura felt perspiration wetting her palms under her gloves. She'd done well, felt confident of her ability to continue. If only it wasn't Kevin she was competing against, if only she didn't feel his eyes staring into her back. She'd never expected it would end like this—just the two of them in the ring, pitting against themselves against each other.

For an instant she almost wished she hadn't come this far. Then immediately she forced the thought from her mind. No, this *was* what she'd set out to achieve all summer. The blue ribbon was within her reach. It would be hers! The jumps were ready. She was motioned to begin.

Putting all else from her mind, she collected Blackfire once again. This was a test of endurance for the mare, her fourth round over an increasingly difficult course. Except for the spots of dampness here and there on the mare's sleek hide, her stress wasn't immediately apparent, but Maura knew she had to be tiring, just as Maura was herself. "One more time, girl," she whispered in the mare's ear. "And this time we're going to win it." Blackfire snorted in understanding, and they were off.

Theirs was a clean course, a beautiful course. All Maura was aware of was the pounding of Blackfire's hooves, the creak of saddle leather, the whistle of the wind past her ears as they cantered and soared, cantered and soared. They took the last fence, clearing with inches to spare.

"Good girl." Maura sighed, patting the mare's neck as she circled and slowed. "Good girl. I'm proud of you."

This time she looked full at Kevin when she left the ring. His green-eyed gaze bit into hers and held. His unbending pride was written clearly in the firm-lipped mouth, the straight set of his shoulders.

Maura was unable to draw her eyes away as he turned and entered the ring. He was talking to Challenger. The stallion's ears flicked back then forward as Kevin urged him into a canter to approach the first fence. They went over magnificently, then went on to the next, and the next. Maura watched for a stumble, a hesitation at the wall, the double bar—nothing. Only perfection. A dead hush had fallen over the spectators. There was a magic about this blending of man and horse, Kevin's powerful will seeming to have injected itself into the stallion so that he lifted himself to greater heights than ever before. They were at the last fence, gathering themselves together, leaping, flying over with incomparable finesse.

There was a moment's silence, then a roar of appreciation from the crowd. So caught up had she been in Kevin's performance, Maura forgot for the moment they were both fighting for the same ribbon. She lifted her hands, too, to join the applause. She was proud of him, of the skill he'd just demonstrated. Her eyes saw the elation on his features; her heart knew what he was feeling.

Then suddenly, as Kevin pulled Challenger down to a trot, the stallion stumbled. Initially it seemed a misstep, a break in stride, but he stumbled again, then again, decidedly favoring his right foreleg.

Frowning, Kevin was quickly off the horse, bending down beside him, examining the leg. The show veterinarian hopped the fence and came striding over.

Kevin already had Challenger's right foreleg in his hands, checking the shoe to see if a bit of stone was lodged there, then pressing his hands gently over the stallion's leg, feeling for heat, for swelling. When the vet reached his side, Kevin turned the examination over to his competent hands.

Only a low rumble of speculation could be heard now in the stands. Kneeling with his back toward her, Kevin's face was unreadable. Had the stallion fractured a leg? Not Challenger, Kevin's pride and joy. The concerned looks in the crowd seemed to echo her worst fears.

The vet finally rose, shaking his head negatively.

Maura took one look at Kevin's face and wanted to cry.

Kevin and the vet spoke together for a moment, then turned and motioned for one of the judges. The three conferred, then the judge returned to the stand and spoke to his fellow judges.

Maura waited tensely, her eyes glued to Kevin's back.

"Ladies and gentlemen. May I have your attention. Mr. DeAngelo is conceding by default, the result of a pulled tendon on Challenger. My fellow judges and I would like to commend both riders on their excellent performances. The winner in the open jumping competition is Miss Maura Langdon on Blackfire of Warren Farms."

Maura felt dazed, unable to comprehend it all. She'd won—but in a way so different from her expectations.

As the applause began in the stands, Maura trotted Blackfire forward to the judges' stand. The mare, sensing the human cheers were in praise of her, arched her neck to a higher angle and lifted her hooves in a jaunty trot. The crowd cheered louder.

Facing the stands as the blue ribbon was fastened to Blackfire's bridle, Maura saw Kevin at the top of the ring, beginning to lead Challenger away. What was he thinking? What was he feeling? The utter defeat she would have known had she lost? Or did he feel bitterness? Anger at this bad stroke of luck? He was assured second place in the event, yet she knew that meant nothing to him now. It was more than a ribbon that stood between them—it was their battle of prides. She had won, and she was sure he despised her for it.

Already, before the blue was secure on

Blackfire's bridle, Kevin was leaving the ring leading his lamed stallion. He'd never once looked in her direction. There would be no congratulations from him, no happiness at her victory. They were further apart than ever.

Suddenly her victory seemed hollow. What was a blue ribbon but a bit of satin? As she watched Kevin walk away, she felt sad and empty.

Chapter 20

Before Maura could leave the ring, friends and acquaintances flocked around her. Alex was practically glowing.

"I knew we could do it. Maura, you were magnificent! Regardless if you won by default. You've had less experience than Kevin, yet you rode him stride for stride. And my dear Blackfire. What a horse!"

"And what a day this has been for the farm!" Lorna added.

Jill wrapped her arms around Maura. Her voice was quiet as she spoke into Maura's ear. "I know what you went through this afternoon, buddy...but things will work out. I know they will. Just think of the future you've got riding.

If you could have heard what they were saying about you! Even the old riding set was saying there was a new light in competitive jumping—you, Maura."

"You're just trying to make me feel better," Maura answered.

"No, she's not." Alex had caught the last words. "As I once mentioned, the National Horse Show is well within your reach. And let me add that I'm extremely proud of you, of my mare, of what you've both done for the reputation of Warren Farm. It's fine consolation for all the years of hard work Lorna and I have put in. After today, it all seems worth it.

"So let's celebrate. A night on the town for my lovely wife and two charming young ladies. The Standish House for dinner and later ice cream at Martin's. We'll leave this crowd to the help that's been hired to take care of them. What do you say, Maura, Jill?"

"Sounds great," exclaimed Jill, reaching for Bill Peter's hand. "Can Bill come, too?"

"Of course. And Maura can feel free to invite anyone she'd like. My night to treat after such a glorious weekend."

To everyone's surprise, though she bowed her head in appreciation to Alex and Lorna, Maura spoke somberly. "Thank you, all of you, but would you really mind if I stayed here? I'm tired. I just feel I need to be alone for a while. The rest of you go out and have a good time."

Maura felt an arm around her shoulder and looked over to see Lorna studying her face. "My dear, of course we understand. While we've been standing on the sidelines, you've had a full workout. Go to the barn, curry Blackfire, then relax. We'll talk about a celebration tomorrow night, or the next."

"Do you mind?"

"Not at all."

"Thank you." Maura was too emotionally and physically exhausted to think of anything but escaping and being by herself for a while.

As the Warrens looked after her, Maura led Blackfire off, deliberately ignoring the crowds that swarmed around her. She brought the mare into the side orchard, through the gate hidden by a row of hedge, out of eyeshot.

She'd won; she should have felt elated. Everything she'd worked for that summer had come to fruition. But she felt empty. In her mind's eye all she could see was the look of heartbreaking disappointment on Kevin's face as he'd left the ring with his lame horse.

In the back of her mind she'd held on to a hope that it would end differently, but it was over now. There was no hope of a reconciliation. Everything between Kevin and her was destroyed forever.

For half an hour she walked Blackfire through the pasture cooling her, then when Maura could stand no more of the inner turmoil, she took the mare back to the barn. Perhaps there would be others there to take her mind off herself.

But she was alone when she led Blackfire into the hay-smelling enclosure. Fastening the mare in the crossties nearest her stall, Maura removed the already loosened saddle and the bridle and slipped a soft leather halter over Blackfire's head. She brought the tack to the back room, then with brushes, sponge, and a pail of warm water in hand, Maura returned to the mare. In the tackroom she'd found the supply of sugar cubes Jill and she had stashed earlier. She gave Blackfire one now.

"A small reward, girl, for the incredible job you've done today."

The mare nickered in appreciation.

"Tired, aren't you? Me, too. But you'll get your feed soon and can relax."

Maura began sponging the mare, then took a sweat strap to remove the excess moisture. She'd found a soft cloth and was rubbing it over Blackfire's coat when she heard footsteps behind her. Thinking it was Charlie, the stableman, she didn't turn. Moments of silence passed, then a voice.

"Maura."

She swung around. She could barely believe she was hearing that familiar, deep voice.

Kevin came forward until he was standing a few feet away.

"Do you mind if I talk to you for a minute, Maura?"

"No . . . of course not. I—I was just brushing down Blackfire."

"So I see."

Maura looked hesitantly at Kevin, wondering, after their weeks of coolness to each other, what had brought him here.

"I wanted to congratulate you, Maura. That

was a beautiful piece of riding. I realize I left the ring in a huff, but I was concerned about Challenger—and disappointed, too."

"How is he?"

"Fine, or will be in a few days. The vet says it's no more than a sprain."

"I felt so bad for you. You probably would have taken the ribbon if it hadn't happened."

"Do you think so, Maura?"

"I tried my best. I wanted to win."

"And deserved to win. I was watching you. You were perfect. Though I admit if I'd continued, I would have run Challenger into the ground to beat you."

"I felt the same."

"Maybe it's better this way then. There are no hard feelings on my part—and there'll be other shows."

She nodded. "I didn't want you for my enemy."

His brows lifted momentarily. "I'm glad of that. Maura, there's something else I want to talk to you about." He paused. "To make a long story short—us."

"Us?"

"We have to talk. I've been doing some deep thinking, swallowing a little pride. I want to be friends again. I've had trouble sleeping at night, thinking that I'll never see that warm smile of yours, never hear you reminding me what an egotistical snob I am, never again see you clearing the high fences. Maura, I don't want it to end with this summer. I like you too much for that. I don't want you to walk away having the

161

wrong impression of me. But I don't want to push you, either. I know I'm older and have been around a lot more than you, but could we shake hands and start all over? I'd like to write to you in the fall, and I'd like it if you'd answer my letters. Do you think you could agree to that?"

Maura's heart started beating faster. She couldn't believe it—this was the last thing she'd expected. The empty space inside her to which she'd begun to grow accustomed in the last weeks, didn't feel so empty anymore.

"Could you, Maura?" he repeated when she didn't immediately answer. "Or do you dislike me that much?"

"No, No—I mean yes—yes. No, I don't dislike you, and yes, if you write, I'll be glad to answer. Oh, Kevin."

Suddenly it was all too much for Maura's self control—the hectic weekend, the mental and physical demands of the competition, the feelings she'd held inside for too long. Tears glistened in her eyes as she reached out to grab Kevin's extended hands and feel his warm fingers close around hers.

"I've wanted to talk to you for so long," she said weakly, "but didn't know how. How was I to explain that you frightened me, that I didn't know what I wanted, that I'd never had any experience with love before. How could I have said all that without seeming like a stupid baby to you? You're so mature, Kevin. You seem to know where you're going, seem to know what you want. When you asked me to go with you and I said no, I only meant I wasn't ready to make that decision—not that I didn't want to see you again. Then you showed up with Justine—"

"Only to hurt you, Maura, as much as you were hurting me. I'm very sorry now."

"Oh, I've been miserable. If we could try it again..."

"We'll try it again." A smile of delight crossed his face. "Oh, Maura, I didn't know what you'd do when I walked in here. I just knew I had to come. I've missed you so much."

"Me, too."

His hands squeezed hers more tightly. "I'll be leaving for Harvard next week. I don't know how much longer you'll be here, but I want to see you again before I leave. And I was thinking maybe, if things work out all right, we could get together at Thanksgiving or Christmas."

"I'd like that."

His eyes stared into hers. "Do you mean that? You're not just saying it to sap me off?"

"I mean it."

His hands reached up to her shoulders. "This time I'll ask first—can I kiss you?"

Maura didn't hesitate. "Yes."

Then Kevin's lips were on hers in a warm, sweet kiss of forgiveness for past pain, appreciation of today, and a promise for tomorrow. Maura was tempted once to draw away, to tell him more of her newly unleashed feelings, but his lips whispered, "Wait," as his arms closed tightly around her.

Blackfire nickered in the background, and her nose gently brushed her mistress's shoulder in approval.

hard-working Jeff and handsome, budding rock star Skip. Which will make her happy?

LITTLE SISTER by Yvonne Greene

Cindy's beautiful older sister, Christine, gets all the cute boys. Cindy just can't win. Then she meets Ron, the best actor in high school. This time Cindy is Number One. But when Christine is chosen to play opposite Ron in the school production of *Romeo and Juliet*, Cindy must prove that she's not second best in Ron's heart.

CALIFORNIA GIRL by Janet Quin-Harkin

Jennie is an outsider in her new Texas home. She is determined to be an Olympic swimmer, but in Texas, all anyone cares about is football. Mark was a high school football star . . . until his accident. But Jennie has fallen in love with his artistic soul and secretly enters his drawings in a contest. Overnight, Mark is a star again. But he may be leaving Jennie behind. Is Jennie losing her love *and* her olympic dream?

GREEN EYES by Suzanne Rand

Dan is one of the most popular boys in school and really cares for Julie. But every time Julie sees Dan so much as talk to another girl, she becomes hopelessly jealous. Then Dan's old girlfriend returns and Julie is convinced that Dan is seeing her again, though Dan assures her he's not. Will Julie let her jealousy ruin the best relationship she's ever had?

THE THOROUGHBRED by Joanna Campbell

Things have always come easily for Maura—her parents are rich, she's pretty, and she's brilliant at horseback riding. Then Maura meets Kevin, a dark, handsome boy, and falls in love for the first time. But Kevin wants too much from her too soon and she's scared. Feeling rejected, Kevin decides to show Maura up in a riding competition. But Maura is determined to win even if she loses her first love doing so.

(Read all of these great Sweet Dreams romances, available wherever Bantam Books are sold.)